THE LEFTOVERS

'Right,' said Mr Steele. 'If I call your name, you're in. If I don't, you're out. Clear?'

Everyone replied together. 'Yes, sir.'

Seth was one of the lads at the side of the pitch. Thirty Year Sevens were standing in their football kits, trying out for the school team. Only sixteen places. You didn't need to be amazing at maths to know this wasn't going to work out well for everyone.

Seth wasn't feeling confident. One of the other kids, Daniel Logan, had given him a massive kick in the knee, and it had *really* hurt. He should've come off, but he hadn't. Seth had to make the team. He'd *always* made the team. He rubbed his sore knee and glanced over at Logan. He was probably the best player of the lot. Blue eyes. Hair like Justin Bieber. Purple boots with an orange tick like the ones Christiano Ronaldo wore. Seth's dad wouldn't let him get multi-coloured boots. He said they were for poseurs.

3

Seth's boots were Nike. Black with a white tick. Plain. Simple. Boring.

Logan smirked at Seth.

Seth looked away, burning with anger.

'Stand behind me if you get called,' Steele said. He looked down at his clipboard. Mr Steele was a short, stocky man with no neck. He reminded Seth of Nigel, a pitbull who belonged to his elderly neighbour, Mrs Mulligan. His bald head was round like the football under his foot and his shorts were way too short – like the ones footballers wore back in ancient times, when they all had big perms and drank beer at half-time. Seth wondered whether Steele used to have a perm. He wouldn't dare ask. No way. Scary stories had reached Seth about Steele before he'd even started at Thomas Moon High School. One was that Steele had shouted at a boy so loud that the boy had peed his pants. Now Seth had met Steele, he thought that was probably true.

'Boyle. Lloyd. Mendes.'

Three of the lads made their way through the crowd and stood behind Steele. They smiled and patted each other on the back. It was his first week at high school so Seth didn't know them. It didn't matter. He didn't like them. The back patting and grinning was well annoying.

Seth's mates, Beefy and Angelo, were standing next to him.

Angelo smiled and shrugged as if to say, 'It's cool. Plenty of time yet.'

Beefy just shook his head.

'Eastwood. Hooper. Ivory.'

Three other lads stepped forward.

'Please say Hart. Please say Hart.' Seth repeated the words over and over in his head. 'And Blood. And Carter.' Seth Hart. Cole "Beefy" Blood. Angelo Carter. They were awesome surnames. They'd have looked great on the back of a school football shirt. Better than stupid Hooper.

Steele called out five more names.

Seth counted the boys behind Steele. Eleven. Sixteen minus eleven. He looked up at the sky as he worked it out. Five places left.

He looked around at the other lads who hadn't had their names called. There were some decent players. Sam Wall was built like, well, a wall. He could've just stood there on his own whenever the opposition had a free kick. Ryo Yoshida was small and nippy. Jordan McGrath was skilful, fast, good at passing and tackling. He looked almost as scary as Mr Steele though. He had a buzz cut which was covered in lots of little scars, and lines cut into his right eyebrow. He looked like someone had dragged his head across the car park. Seth wouldn't be mentioning that to Jordan either.

They weren't all good though. There was Alan Block too. He was a tragedy. Every time the ball came anywhere near him, he squeezed his eyes shut like he was terrified of it. Who was scared of footballs? Mrs Mulligan and cats, that's who. If Seth had to give Alan a weirdo rating out of ten, he'd give him an eight. Maybe even a nine.

'Hawks,' said Steele.

Four places left.

'Foreman.'

Seth felt a lump grow in his throat. He looked over at his mates again.

Angelo's grin had shrunk a little.

Beefy was staring down at the grass.

'Walters.'

One of them definitely hadn't got in.

'Ford,' said Steele.

Two of them hadn't got in. Seth wasn't even sure he wanted to get in now. Not if it meant playing without his best mates.

'Logan,' said Steele. 'And that's your lot. If I didn't call your name out, you weren't good enough.'

Seth's heart sank to the pit of his stomach. This had meant everything and now it was all coming crashing down around him. What was he going to tell his dad? He felt sick. He took a breath and steadied himself. The smell of the freshly cut grass filled his lungs.

'Knew it,' said Beefy. 'We were never getting in.'

'Nah, man,' said Angelo. 'We're as good as any of them over there. Don't you reckon, Seth?'

Seth looked over. The players Steele had picked were mainly athletic, good-looking and skilful. They looked like they'd been made in a factory. All of them were shaking hands and patting backs. Idiots. Logan was the biggest idiot of the lot.

Sam, Ryo and most of the other lads who hadn't been picked began to walk off.

Steele stood there, studying his clipboard.

Seth took a breath and approached the PE teacher. 'Sir?' he said.

'What?' snapped Steele.

'Erm, I was just wondering... where me and my mates went wrong?' Seth gestured to Beefy and Angelo with a flick of his head.

Steele glanced at them and sniffed. He pointed at Beefy with his pen. 'Fat,' he said. Then Angelo. 'Liability.' He gave Seth a look. 'Too slow.' Then he pointed at Jordan, who was sitting on the grass taking off his boots. 'Trouble. Happy?'

Seth looked around at his mates. They didn't look happy at all.

Jordan dumped his boots in his bag. He pulled on a pair of battered Adidas Superstars, picked himself up and sloped away.

'Can we try again?' asked Seth.

'No,' said Steele. 'If I were you, I'd give up football. Have a go at something else. Dancing or... knitting...'

Seth felt his heart sink even further. It was somewhere around his bum now.

Steele turned around to his brand-new team. 'Well done lads,' he said. 'You lot are the wheat. The good stuff. Those lot are the chaff.' He pointed a thumb over his shoulder.

'What's "chaff"?' asked Luke Foreman. He was one of the biggest kids in the year. He had short hair and a forehead like a caveman's. He looked like he'd been in the gym lifting weights since he was three.

'The chaff's the leftovers, son,' said Steele. 'The bit you don't want.'

'Are they the freaks then, sir?' asked Logan.

'The PC brigade wouldn't approve of us saying that,' said Steele. 'But yes. They're the freaks.'

The new team laughed.

More back patting, more shaking hands and now laughing at the players who didn't make the team. Seth hated them all. They were TOTAL idiots.

'Does he know we can hear him?' Beefy asked Seth.

'Don't reckon he cares,' said Seth.

Angelo balled his fists.

Seth put his hand on Angelo's shoulder and eased him away. 'Let's do one,' he said.

The three of them trudged across the grass towards the school gates. Seth winced a little as he put weight on his knee. He looked back over his shoulder.

Logan was watching them go, grinning. Slowly, he mouthed the word 'freaks'.

Seth looked away. He wanted to go back and say something to Logan. Hit him with an awesome comeback. Like, 'You're the freak, freak,' or 'Freak off, freakbag.' OK, they weren't awesome comebacks. What he really wanted to do was go over and thump him in the gut. Or stamp on his knee, the way Logan had stamped on his. But what could he do? He had Angelo and Beefy backing him up. Logan had the whole school team.

The lads headed home.

'I liked it better at Milton Hall,' said Angelo. 'This place sucks.'

Milton Hall was the primary school the boys had just left. Seth nodded. Milton Hall *was* better. At Milton Hall, they were all on the school team, the teachers didn't call them 'freaks' and there weren't any idiots like Logan.

Seth had been best mates with Beefy and Angelo since forever. They'd all met at nursery. One of Seth's first memories was of Angelo saving him from a girl who'd pushed him over. She'd wanted to ride around in the same toy police car. He'd been flat on the ground when Angelo came to his rescue. All he saw was Angelo's big afro and his skinny arms and legs. 'Get off him!' he'd shouted. Then he'd shoved the girl over too. Angelo hadn't changed much. He still had the skinny arms and legs, but now his hair was braided in cornrows. And he hadn't shoved any girls over for a while, which was good.

Beefy had been in their class too, winning them over instantly with a never-ending supply of sweets. Whatever the occasion, Beefy had the goodies. Gum, sweets, chocolates. He was like Willy Wonka. Except less weird. He hadn't changed much either. He was still chunky, with freckles and short blonde hair. And he still had a never-ending supply of sweets.

Seth thought it was only him that'd really changed. He'd been chunky too when he was little. And he was the shortest. But he was slim now and taller than his mates. He still had the same short, mousy hair though. He wondered whether he'd have the same hairstyle for the rest of his life.

The lads walked on past the garage and shops, stopping at the corner of Seth's street.

'We just giving up then?' asked Beefy.

Seth looked at his friends. They were as gutted as he could ever remember seeing them. Even Angelo's grin had almost slipped completely off his face.

It wasn't right. Why should they give up something they loved just because of some old bully in ridiculously tight shorts? Seth remembered Mr Steele's face as he'd delivered the 'too slow' verdict. It was like he was enjoying himself. Like he loved being a miserable old fart to kids.

'No,' said Seth, shaking his head. 'We won't give up.'

'But...'

Seth interrupted Beefy before he could finish. 'I don't care what that old fart-bag says!'

Angelo sniggered. 'Fart-bag.'

'We love football don't we?' asked Seth.

Beefy and Angelo looked at each other. It was a no-brainer.

They both nodded.

'You don't give up things you love,' Seth insisted. He was fired up now. It was like he was giving a speech at the end of a film. Suddenly he knew what he wanted to do about it all.

'True,' said Beefy, 'but my mum should've given up cakes ages ago!'

They all creased up.

'How can we play when we don't have a team to play for?' asked Angelo. 'Work that one out, Sherlock.'

Seth fixed them with a determined stare. 'We start our own team,' he said.

TEAM MEETING

Seth lived on a quiet street with lots of trees. There were lots of dogs too. And old ladies. He put his key in the front door and let the three of them in.

Once they'd dumped their bags and kicked off their trainers, they all plodded up the stairs to Seth's bedroom and flopped onto his bed. Seth sighed, rolled down his socks and pulled off his shin-guards.

Beefy picked up a controller and turned the Xbox on.

Angelo picked up the other controller.

After a moment, the *FIFA* intro music started playing.

Seth looked around his room. His wallpaper was United. His duvet cover was United. His curtains. His clock. Even his teddy. It was like being in the Megastore. As much as he didn't want to think about football right now, it was everywhere he looked. It *was* his life. He felt sick all over again.

'Put something else on,' said Seth.

'But we wanna play this,' said Beefy. 'I owe him an ass kicking!'

'Yeah right!' said Angelo. 'You couldn't kick anyone's ass. You couldn't even kick a baby's ass!'

'You wish,' said Beefy.

'I wish you could kick a baby's ass?' asked Angelo. 'Err, why would I...'

'JUST TURN IT OFF!' shouted Seth.

'All right, man, chill,' said Angelo. He got up and turned the console off.

The three of them sat there in silence.

There was a knock at the door and after a moment, Seth's dad came into the room. 'How'd it go then?' he asked.

Seth's dad was tall and wide. He was easily over six foot and at the last weigh-in, he was over sixteen stone. His hair was short – number one – and he had a tanned face. He had on a paint-splattered T-shirt and a pair of scruffy old jeans. He was a builder. He even had a builder's name – Steve. In fact, he was builder-tastic. He worked outside a lot of the time. It had some benefits; getting big, having a nice tan. But Seth's dad was out there in the rain and snow.

Seth was pretty sure that must suck. His dad had a weights bench in the garage. Seth sat and watched him do bench presses sometimes. He was ridiculously strong. Like Thor. Except he didn't speak in that stupid old English. And he didn't have long blonde hair. And the hammer in his toolbox wasn't magic and didn't have its own name. Actually, he was nothing like Thor. But he *was* strong. And tough too. He was a black belt in jiu-jitsu.

'We're the leftovers,' said Angelo.

'The "Freaks",' said Beefy.

Steve frowned and scratched his forehead. 'You what?'

Seth sat up on his bed. 'That's what Steele called us.'

'He called you freaks?' asked Steve.

Seth shrugged.

'I'm not having that.'

'What you gonna do?' asked Seth.

'I'm gonna see this bloke and have a word.'

'Are you gonna give him a karate chop?' asked Angelo.

'Maybe,' Steve shrugged.

'Just leave it, Dad,' said Seth. He didn't want his dad to go down to the school and karate-kick Steele's head off. OK, maybe he did. A bit. Maybe even more than a bit. But he didn't want his dad to get in trouble. He didn't want to get in trouble either. If his dad went and had a pop at Steele, everyone would be talking about them. That was the last thing he wanted at a new school.

'No, Seth,' said Steve. 'It's not on. He shouldn't be saying things like that.'

'Doesn't matter anyway,' said Beefy. 'We're starting our own team.'

Steve frowned. 'Your own team?'

'Why not?' asked Seth.

'How's that gonna work?'

'We'll get some other lads who didn't get in,' said Seth. 'We'll... we'll organise matches and that.'

Steve sniffed and nodded. 'OK. Well, you sound like you know what you're doing. I'll leave you to it.' He left the room.

'You should've let him go down to school, mate,' said Angelo. 'Steele deserves it.'

Seth didn't argue.

'How we gonna get our team going then?' asked Beefy.

'How about a team meeting?' Seth suggested. 'Like, now.'

'Sounds sweet,' said Angelo. 'We probably need pens.'

'And paper,' said Beefy.

'In the drawer over there.' Seth pointed over

at his desk.

Angelo leapt across the room. After a bit of a rummage, he came back with a notepad and some felt-tip pens and handed them over.

'Now what?' asked Beefy.

They looked around at each other.

'Shall we go and ask your dad?' asked Angelo.

Seth's living room had a wooden floor which he liked to slide around on when he was in a good mood. There was no sliding today though. There was red wallpaper on one of the walls, which Seth had picked. It was the same wall where his dad had hung his United shirt that'd been signed by the double winning team. It was his dad's most treasured possession. Seth's mum had bought it for him. That was years ago, when Seth was little. Before his mum had died of cancer.

Steve was sitting in his chair reading a paper and taking a slurp from a cup of tea. He looked up and nodded.

The three mates plonked themselves on the sofa.

'Your tea's on, Seth,' he said. 'What about you lot? You want anything?'

Angelo shook his head. 'I'm good, thanks, Stevie,' he said.

Beefy shook his head too.

Steve frowned. 'What's the matter, Beef? Not like you to turn down food?'

'I'm OK,' said Beefy. 'Just not hungry.'

'Is it because of what Steele said?' asked Angelo.

'What else did he say?' asked Steve.

'He said Beefy was fat,' Angelo replied. 'And he said Seth was slow. And I was a liable-something?'

'A liability,' said Seth.

'What does that even mean?' asked Angelo.

'It means you'll try and strangle someone for tackling you!' said Seth.

Angelo grinned.

'You sure you don't want me to go down that school?' asked Steve.

Seth shook his head. 'Nah, Dad, it's all right.'

'You want some tea, Beef, you have some tea. OK?' said Steve.

'OK, Steve,' said Beefy. A hint of a smile appeared on his face. 'I'll think about it.'

'Dad, what do you do at a team meeting?' asked Seth.

'Well, when I meet with the boys, it usually involves a few pints,' said Steve.

'Sounds good,' said Angelo, nodding. 'You get the round in, Big Steve.'

Steve smirked and sat up in his armchair.

'When you're all eighteen,' he said. 'But not a day before. What about a team name? Seems like a good place to start.'

'Ninjas FC!' said Angelo.

'*Really?*' asked Seth.

'Why not?' Angelo shrugged. 'We can dress like ninjas.' He pulled his hands into a karate guard. 'That's the way you do it, innit, Steve? And everyone will be proper scared when we play them!' He chopped Beefy on the thigh.

'Oi!' said Beefy. 'Get off!'

'That's dumb,' said Seth.

'What about United?' asked Beefy.

'That's it?' asked Seth. 'United?'

'Yeah,' said Beefy. 'Just like United. What do you think?'

'I think you have the imagination of a tree trunk,' said Seth. 'And United aren't just called "United" are they?'

Angelo nodded. 'It sucks.'

'You both suck,' said Seth. Then an idea bounced into his brain. 'What about Freaks United?'

Beefy and Angelo looked at each other.

'Don't get it,' said Angelo.

'Well that's what that Steele and Logan called us,' said Seth. 'They said we were freaks. So what if we are? And what if everyone else who plays for us is a freak too?'

'I don't know,' said Beefy. He screwed his face up like he was eating a Haribo Sour.

'Yeah, me neither,' said Angelo. He screwed his face up too.

'I think it's the best one,' said Seth.

'Why don't you have a think on it?' said Steve. He smiled as he looked down at his paper. 'So who's gonna coach you? You'll need a coach, unless you want to do it yourselves.'

It was Seth's turn to screw his face up. The idea of running around in short shorts, blowing whistles and shouting at kids wasn't cool. He looked at Angelo. Angelo raised his eyebrows. Then he looked at Beefy. Beefy nodded. Seth knew exactly what they were thinking.

'Daaad,' said Seth.

'Whaaat?' asked Steve.

'Would you coach us?'

Steve played five-a-side with his mates every week. Seth often went along to watch. His dad was a good player. He scored loads of goals. And he knew more about football than anyone else Seth had ever met.

'Yeah, Big Stevie, will you?' asked Angelo.

'Go on,' said Beefy.

'All right, lads, give me a chance,' said Steve. He took a breath and inflated his cheeks. After a moment, he forced the air out of his mouth, making a fart noise.

Angelo sniggered.

'Go on then,' said Steve.

'Really?' asked Seth.

'As long as you do what I say,' said Steve. 'Any messing about and that's it. OK?'

'OK,' said Seth.

Now Seth was feeling pretty excited.

'You'll need to find me some more players, though,' Steve said.

'We'll ask some of the other lads who didn't get in,' said Beefy. 'See if they're up for it?'

Seth thought about some of the other lads who didn't get in – Sam, Ryo, Jordan – he didn't fancy going up to them and asking them if they wanted to play for some no-name team. He didn't even know them. 'Can you imagine going up to Jordan McGrath and asking him anything?' asked Seth.

'He'd probably head-butt us!' said Angelo.

'OK, then,' said Steve. 'How about this? You make a poster? Stick it up on the notice board at school, then whoever wants to, can come along?'

Beefy and Angelo nodded.

'Good plan,' said Seth.

'You see, son,' said Steve. 'Your dad's more than just a pretty face.' He winked at Seth.

'As if you've got a pretty face!' said Seth.

'So what's for tea, then, Steve?' asked Beefy.

Seth and Angelo burst out laughing.

Seth and his mates got into school the following morning and headed for the foyer. There were loads of kids and teachers around.

'You gonna put it up then?' asked Beefy.

Seth glanced around. 'Not yet,' he said. 'Let's wait until the coast's clear.'

The boys stood under the main stairs until the bell rang out for registration. Once the foyer had cleared, they scurried over to the notice board.

Seth unzipped his backpack and pulled out the rolled-up poster they'd made the night before. He unrolled it and held it in place.

Angelo went to pull the drawing pins out of the corner of the notice board.

'Let Beefy do it,' said Seth.

'Why?' asked Angelo. 'Don't you trust me?'

'Not with anything sharp. No.'

Angelo sucked his teeth.

Beefy pulled a couple of drawing pins from the notice board and stuck one in each corner of the poster.

The boys stood back.

'Looks good,' said Angelo.

Seth nodded. It did look good. It said:

DO YOU LOVE FOOTBALL?
Do you want to play for
an awesome new team?
If you do, we will be meeting on:
Wednesday 12th September at 6.30 pm
at Barrowby Field
Thank you for your time!

It was lunch time. After Seth and Angelo had waited for Beefy to get through his humongous meal, they went back to the foyer and hung about under the main stairs. It was the perfect place to see if anyone was showing interest in their poster.

'D'you think anyone's seen it?' asked Beefy. His mouth was filled with Mars bar.

'Dunno,' said Seth. 'Hope so.'

Just then Steele appeared from the staff room. The boys watched, hunched low, as he walked over to the notice board. He stood with his hands behind his back and studied the poster.

'Uh-oh,' said Angelo.

Steele had a shifty glance around. Then he unpinned the poster, ripped it in half and dropped the pieces in a bin as he walked away.

Seth blinked. He couldn't believe it. 'No way!

Did you just see that?' There was a lump in his throat. His eyes started stinging. 'He... he can't do that. Can he?'

Beefy swallowed down his Mars bar and nodded.

Seth wished he'd set his dad on Steele now. He felt angry and embarrassed and helpless. What could they do? It wasn't right. Seth looked at his mates. 'No way I'm having that,' he said. 'Steele just started a war. You two with me?'

TRY OUTS

Seth, his dad and the boys waited over on the playing fields near Seth's house. They were all standing on the football pitch next to a set of goalposts. Over to the right, but some way off, was a kids' play area. It had a little fence around it and a swing, a climbing frame and a see-saw. Above them the sky was powder blue. The sun was still shining. It was a nice, warm evening. Perfect for a kick-about.

'Do you think anyone will show up?' asked Steve.

'Doubt it,' said Seth. 'Not after Steele ripped our poster up.'

Steve shook his head. 'The offer's still there, lads. You want me to go down that school, just say the word.'

Seth thought about Steele ripping their poster down. He felt himself growing hot with anger all over again. He was calmer now though. 'It's

25

cool, Dad,' he said. 'It doesn't matter.' Seth didn't really believe that though. It did matter. But his dad getting into trouble wouldn't be a good move.

'Who's that?' asked Beefy. He pointed towards the play area.

Seth looked across the field.

There were a few kids approaching on bikes.

As they got closer, Seth realised it was Logan and a few of the lads who'd been picked for the school team.

'Why would they want to play with us?' asked Angelo. 'They're on the school team.'

Logan and his mates stopped behind the goalposts.

'Have you come for training?' asked Angelo.

Logan laughed. 'As if. We've come to have a laugh!'

His mates started laughing too.

Seth's heart sank. It wasn't quite at his bum, but it wasn't far away. New school – new start. And they were about to make right donkeys of themselves.

Steve turned around to Logan and his mates. 'You all right there, boys?' he asked.

Logan and his mates stopped laughing.

'GUYS! GUYS!' shouted someone from across the field.

Seth looked over towards the kids' play area again. Someone else was running towards them.

'Who's that?' asked Beefy.

Seth squinted.

Whoever it was, he was wearing a Scooby Doo T-shirt and black tracksuit pants with a solitary white stripe.

'Oh no,' said Seth.

'Who is it?' asked Angelo.

'It's Alan Block,' said Seth.

'Who?' asked Angelo.

'That one who was scared of the ball,' said Seth. 'From the try-outs.'

Alan raced onto the pitch and joined the boys. He was panting and out of breath. He was podgy, with cheeks like a hamster's. He had tiny eyes and ginger hair.

Logan and his mates were laughing all over again.

'This gets better and better,' said Logan. 'Come on, boys, let's leave these freaks to it.'

Logan and his mates left, still laughing.

'I'm sorry... I'm late,' said Alan, as he panted. 'I was videoing... my cat...'

'Why were you videoing your cat?' asked Seth.

'He was talking,' said Alan.

Steve frowned.

'Who are you?' Alan asked Steve.

27

'I'm Seth's dad. Steve,' said Steve

'You're handsome,' said Alan. 'Are you a singer?'

Steve's frown was replaced with a smile. He shook his head. 'Only in the shower,' he said.

'Oh,' said Alan. He sounded quite surprised. He turned to Seth and the others. 'So what's the team called?' asked Alan.

'We don't have a name yet,' said Seth.

'I wanted Ninjas FC,' said Angelo.

Alan's eyes grew wider. 'I love ninjas!'

'I wanted Freaks United,' said Seth.

'I like freaks too!' said Alan. 'Did you know that in the old days they used to make freaks?'

'Make freaks?' asked Beefy. 'What you on about?'

'Freaks were big business back then,' said Alan. 'They used to put people in vases and stuff so they'd grow all weird.'

'I think he's grown all weird,' Seth whispered to Beefy.

Beefy sniggered.

'So is this us then?' asked Steve.

'Looks like it,' said Seth.

'Right, first things first,' said Steve. 'Stretches.'

'Ooh,' said Alan. 'Before I forget.' He dug into the pockets of his tracksuit pants and pulled out a few small cards. He handed one to everyone.

TRY OUTS

Seth studied the card. It said:

Name: Alan Block
Twitter: @theonlyalanblock
Website: www.alanblockstuff.com
Address: 66 Cuckoo Street,
Middle Town, MI5 6IQ
Skills: drawing cats, videoing cats,
line dancing, graphic design

Seth blinked a few times. Then frowned. Alan Block's weirdo rating was officially at ten.

Steve shook his head when he read the card and slipped it into his pocket. 'Right then, lads,' he said. 'Couple of stretches first. I don't want you picking up any injuries. Especially not you, Alan, if you've got your line dancing...'

'Good point!' said Alan.

'Follow my lead,' said Steve. He put his left hand on the back of his neck. He grabbed his left elbow with his right hand and pulled it. 'Stretch then, lads. Come on.'

The lads moaned, then copied what Steve was doing.

'Can you feel that?' asked Steve.

'Yes, Dad,' said Seth. 'It's amazing.'

'Less of the lip, kidda,' said Steve. 'Now switch sides.'

Everyone followed Steve's lead again.

'Right, lads, now some star jumps,' said Steve. He started doing star jumps.

Beefy groaned.

The boys started doing star jumps too.

'Stevie, I don't mean to be rude,' said Angelo. 'But this isn't fun.'

'I never said it would be fun,' said Steve. 'NOW JUMP!' he shouted.

The lads jumped.

After the star jumps, they did press ups. Then sit-ups. Squats. Lunges.

Every time Alan lunged, his tracksuit pants came down a bit further. He had on polka-dot boxers. 'Sorry,' he said. He pulled his pants up.

Then it happened again.

And again.

Seth thought it was funny at first, but he could only take so much of Alan Block's butt.

Steve put them through their paces until they were all puffing and panting and sweat was dripping from their noses.

'Right, that's enough warm up,' said Steve. 'Let's play some ball. Bit of two on two. Beefs and Angelo against Seth and Alan. I'll go in between the sticks.' He went over to his huge holdall and unzipped it. He took out a football. Then he positioned himself between the goalposts.

'Me and you then, Seth,' said Alan.

Seth looked at Alan. Then he looked over at Beefy and Angelo.

The pair of them grinned at him.

'Yeah, wicked,' said Seth.

Steve threw the ball out and the boys kicked off.

Seth chased the ball down and brought it under control.

Angelo came charging at him like a rhino.

Seth was never keen on having Angelo charge at him. Steele was harsh, but Angelo *was* a bit of a liability. He looked for Alan and knocked the ball to his partner.

Alan swung his foot at the ball, completely missing it. He had the coordination of a newborn donkey.

Seth groaned.

'SORRY!' shouted Alan.

Alan chased after the ball, but Beefy barged him out of the way no problem. It wasn't a fair contest. It was like The Juggernaut against Pudsey Bear.

Beefy took the ball. He sized up where the goal was and struck one. The ball arrowed into the bottom corner.

Steve dived for it. He stretched out an arm, but Beefy's shot was too good.

The ball smacked the inside of the post with a satisfying THUD.

One-nil to Beefy and Angelo.

Steve picked himself up. 'Goal, Beef,' he said. He went after the ball as it rolled across the grass.

'Yeah, goal, Beef!' repeated Alan.

Seth shook his head.

Steve picked up the ball and gave it a huge boot back onto the pitch.

Angelo raced after it.

Alan too.

Angelo got a hold of the ball.

Alan looked as though he might make a tackle.

'Try it,' said Angelo. 'And I'll strangle you!'

Alan stopped. He looked over at Seth in confusion. 'CAN HE DO THAT? CAN HE STRANGLE ME??'

Seth buried his head in his hands as Angelo raced towards the goal.

Angelo smacked the ball hard.

Two-nil.

And that's how it went. Whenever Seth passed the ball to Alan, Alan either miskicked it or lost it straight away. Seth was pretty sure Alan was the worst footballer he'd ever seen. In fact, he'd seen toddlers with better tekkers. All Seth could do was try and take on Beefy and Angelo on his own. In the end, Seth and Alan lost ten-three. Seth was not impressed.

Steve switched the teams up, but it didn't matter. Whoever got Alan lost. Everyone stopped passing to him in the end. Alan Block was officially pointless.

Once all three boys had had a turn playing with Alan, Steve called an end to the session. 'Well that wasn't so bad, was it, lads?' asked Steve. 'Bit of a workout at least.'

Seth looked around at Angelo and Beefy.

Neither of his mates said a word. They didn't need to. Seth could tell they all thought it had been a fat waste of time.

Beefy pulled a packet of Skittles out of his pocket. He offered them to Seth and Angelo, but left out Alan.

'Same time next week?' asked Steve.

'I'll be here,' said Alan.

'Don't bother,' said Seth.

'Oh,' said Alan. 'OK, then.' He looked down at the ground for a moment. Then he raced away towards the play area, where he'd come from.

'Seth,' said his dad. 'Bit harsh?'

'But he was really crap,' said Seth.

'He was crap, Stevie,' added Angelo.

'He was,' said Steve. 'But he showed up. And from where I'm standing, you lot can't afford to lose any team-mates.'

Seth looked at the others.

Angelo sighed.

Beefy looked at the ground.

'But he was *really* crap,' said Seth. 'We'd never win a game with him playing.'

'You'll never get a game if you don't have enough players,' said Steve.

Seth shrugged. 'I guess,' he said.

'If it was me,' said Steve. 'I'd go and find that weird little lad and ask him to come back next week.'

Seth plodded over to his mates. He pulled Alan's business card out of the pocket of his tracksuit pants. 'Who has a business card, anyway?' he asked.

'Movie stars,' said Angelo. 'And rappers.'

'I don't think Alan Block is either of those,' said Seth.

'What do you think he's got on this website?' asked Angelo.

'Dunno,' said Seth. 'But I'll bet it's weird.'

'How weird?' asked Angelo. 'You don't think he's weird enough to murder people, do you?'

Alan Block was a definite ten on the weird-o-meter. There was no telling what someone with that level of weirdness would do.

'I think we *should* say sorry to him,' said Seth.

Beefy and Angelo nodded.

'Plus I heard his sister's well fit,' Angelo said. 'We should go round his house right now.'

MATCH FIXED

Alan's house wasn't far from the playing fields. Ten minutes walk, tops. The lads didn't say much as they walked.

Seth wasn't sure what the others were thinking, but there were a few thoughts going around in his head. Seeing Logan at school the next day. No one turning up for training. Alan Block stalking them all down and slaying them with an axe.

When they got to Alan's street, Seth started to feel nervous. What if Alan had told his parents what they'd said to him? They might have axes too. Or chainsaws. He didn't know what they were heading into.

Beefy pointed at the street sign. 'Cuckoo Street,' he said.

'Cuckoo Land!' said Angelo, and they both laughed.

Seth did his best to join in.

'These houses all look pretty normal,' said Angelo.

'Yeah, and?' said Beefy.

'Well, I just thought Alan Block would live somewhere weird.'

'Like where?'

'Like a junk yard,' said Angelo. 'Or a big shoe.'

'I think you and Alan Block might be as weird as each other,' Seth told him.

Angelo pushed him in the shoulder.

He was right though, Cuckoo Street was pretty normal. The houses all had nice gardens and nice cars parked outside. Hanging baskets. Privet hedges. It was about as normal as you could get.

Alan lived at number sixty-six. The boys stopped at the end of the driveway. Alan's house was especially normal-looking. It had a red door and a little gnome stood near the front-door step. A zero on the weird-o-meter, which seemed weird.

Seth turned to the other two. 'Who wants to go up?'

'I don't,' said Angelo. 'He might stab me!'

'Why don't we all go?' Beefy suggested.

The lads slowly made their way up Alan's driveway together.

Seth took a breath and pressed Alan's doorbell.

DING. DONG.

Someone shouted from inside.

Then the door opened.

A girl was standing there. She was taller than all of them. She had long dark hair and big brown eyes like something out of a Japanese cartoon. She was wearing jeans and a T-shirt with zombies on it that said *Dawn of the Dead.*

Seth gulped. *Actually* gulped. He recognised her from school. She was in Year Nine. She'd stuck in his head, because he'd thought she was well pretty. Easily an eight on the fit-o-meter. Maybe a nine. Seth glanced at his mates.

Angelo was wearing his usual stupid grin.

Beefy's mouth was hanging open.

Seth thought about reaching over and closing it for him.

'Is... erm... Alan in?' asked Seth.

The girl turned around and shouted, 'ALAN!'

Within seconds, Alan came bounding down the stairs like a podgy kangaroo. He appeared at the door with a huge grin. 'It's OK, sis, I'll take it from here.'

'Okey doke, little bro,' said the girl and she went off into the house.

Seth waited a few seconds before he said anything. 'Is that your sister?' he asked.

Alan nodded.

'She seems nice,' said Beefy.

'She's fit!' said Angelo.

'Shush, man,' said Seth.

'What?' asked Angelo. 'She IS fit.'

'She can run really fast!' said Alan. 'Shall I ask her to show you?'

'No,' said Seth. 'Don't do that.'

'Why not?'

'Yeah, why not?' said Angelo.

'Just don't,' said Seth. 'Anyway, that's not why we're here. We thought we better come over. Say sorry. We were out of order.'

'Yeah. Sorry for threatening to strangle you,' said Angelo.

'Sorry for not offering you some sweets,' added Beefy. He pulled the crumpled packet of Skittles from his pocket and offered them to Alan.

Alan took a few and stuffed them into his mouth.

'You can come and train with us next week, if you like?' said Seth.

'Definitely!' said Alan.

'So we're all good?' asked Seth.

'All good in the hood!' Alan replied. 'That's what they say, isn't it? On the telly? On the music channels? *All good in the hood*?'

Seth frowned. 'I guess.'

'And you won't murder us?' asked Angelo.

'No,' said Alan. 'I won't. Did you think what name you'd call the team? I think you should have a name. I like Freaks United best.'

Seth looked at the others. Then he looked at Alan. 'I think it fits best too,' he said.

'Definitely,' added Beefy.

Angelo made an 'uh-huh' noise.

Seth clapped his hands together like his dad often did. 'Freaks United it is,' he said. 'Sorted. We'll see you at school tomorrow, Alan.'

Alan nodded.

'Oh,' whispered Seth. 'What's your sister's name?'

'Laura,' Alan told them. 'Do you like her?' His grin grew to twice its original size.

'I... erm... I didn't...'

'I do!' said Angelo, interrupting Seth.

'Me too!' said Beefy.

Alan laughed. Then he closed the door.

Seth blinked, then turned to his mates. 'You two are proper idiots.'

'What?' asked Angelo.

'Yeah, what?' asked Beefy.

Seth shook his head.

It was the same time, same place for the next training session a week later. They were all gathered in front of Seth's dad, all in football shirts – except for Alan. He was wearing a T-shirt with a picture of *The Muppets* on it. Animal was playing the drums. Kermit was on the guitar. Miss Piggy was singing. As far as Seth was concerned, Alan could've had a picture of himself on his T-shirt too. He was the biggest muppet of the lot, and Seth had wondered all week about the wisdom of having him back.

'Right then, lads,' said Steve. 'Stretches.'

The boys groaned before they began stretching out their arms and legs.

Once they were done with their sit-ups and press-ups, Steve sat himself down on the grass. 'Take a seat,' he said.

The lads sat down on the grass in front of him.

'I've been thinking,' said Steve. 'We need to focus on individual aspects of your game.'

'You've been playing too much *Football Manager*!' Seth cried.

Beefy and Angelo sniggered.

'What?' asked Steve. 'It's good research. Anyway, like I said, I've been thinking. Seth, what areas of your game do you want to work on?'

Seth thought about what Steele had said to him. 'I'd like to be faster, I guess,' he said.

'Right,' said Steve. 'I want you to work on your sprinting. You've got an extra yard up here...' He tapped his head. 'You just need an extra yard in your legs. What about you, Beef?' asked Steve.

Beefy took a bite from his Bounty. 'I guess I'd like to lose a bit of weight,' he said. He stopped chewing.

Steve reached over and unzipped his holdall. He pulled out some papers and handed them to Beefy, who looked down at them, frowning.

'What're these? Is it a test?'

'No, it's a meal plan and a training regime,' Steve told him.

Beefy looked around, eyes wide with panic.

'Don't worry. Nothing too heavy, just a few pointers.'

Beefy looked over the papers. He tilted his head as if to say 'this isn't too bad.'

'Now, Ange, how about you?'

'I wish I didn't want to strangle people when they tried to tackle me,' said Angelo. 'Sorry, Alan.'

Alan grinned.

Seth's dad pulled a punch-pad and a pair of boxing gloves out of the holdall. 'We can do some work on these. Get some of that rage out of you.'

'Is that holdall magic, Dad?' asked Seth. 'You gonna pull a bunny out next?'

Steve grinned. 'No, smart-arse, I just came

prepared. Alan, what would you like to develop?'

'I'd like to be able to kick the ball, Mr Hart,' said Alan.

The other boys laughed.

Alan looked around. He seemed surprised that he'd made them laugh and he laughed too.

'That's OK, Alan,' Steve said. 'And just call me "Steve".'

'OK, Steve!' said Alan. He sounded pretty excited to be saying 'Steve'. A bit too excited. He was a definite ten on the weird-o-meter. A solid eight on the over-excited-o-meter too.

'You need to work on your ball control,' Steve told him. 'Bit of practice should do it.' He pulled out a ball and rolled it to Alan.

Alan tried to grab the ball, but it rolled by him. He scrambled to his feet and raced after it.

'Maybe a lot of practice,' said Steve.

Steve got the boys working individually. Seth did sprints. Beefy did sit-ups. Angelo pounded the punch pad. Alan tried to do kick-ups. All the time Steve shouted encouragement to them.

'That's it, Seth.'

'Abs of steel, Beef! Come on!'

'Get it all out, Ange!'

'Come on, Alan. Don't be scared of the thing!'

Seth looked around at his team-mates. Each

of them had a smile on their faces.

Beefy was pouring with sweat, but he was showing more determination and effort than Seth had ever seen.

Angelo was sweating too. But he was smiling and he seemed sort of calm.

Alan had managed three consecutive kick-ups.

Even Seth felt that he was sprinting a bit quicker. Maybe his lack of pace was in his head. Maybe it was just that he didn't push himself hard enough? He didn't know. What he did know was that he was having fun and so were his mates. He smiled to himself. Maybe this wasn't such a big fat waste of time after all.

Then he stopped smiling.

About twenty metres away Daniel Logan, Luke Foreman and Sam Mendes were on their BMX bikes and were riding towards them.

Logan had on a pair of cool Air Force Ones. They were blue and black with a yellow tick. Just like the ones Seth had asked his dad for and been told no.

Foreman had on an Adidas T-shirt that was tight around his big body. Most T-shirts would've been tight around Foreman though.

Mendes had bulging blue eyes and blonde, messed-up hair that looked like it took him six hours and a tonne of product to get it to look messy.

Beefy stopped doing his sit-ups.

Angelo stopped pounding the punchpad.

Alan chased after his ball.

'They've still got the Blockster with them,' said Logan from the side of the pitch. 'You lot are *proper* freaks. It's official!' He looked around at his mates and started laughing.

Seth felt hot and itchy. He wanted to dig a hole in the ground and bury himself under the pitch.

Angelo growled.

'Remember what we talked about,' said Seth's dad. 'Counting to ten?'

'Do you want a match?' Alan asked Logan.

Seth was shocked by Alan's boldness, even if his suggestion was utterly terrible.

Logan looked around at his friends and sniggered. 'Get a grip, Blockhead. We'd destroy you.'

'No you wouldn't,' said Angelo.

Seth's heart sank to his bum once again. What were they doing?!

'Go on, then,' said Logan. 'We'll play you. It'll be fun making you look stupider than you already do.'

'If you want a game,' said Steve. 'Let's make

it a proper game. Four weeks from now. Five-a-side. On this pitch.'

'If you want to make it a game,' said Logan. 'We've gotta be talking eleven-a-side.'

Seth's dad looked around at the Freaks and back at Logan. 'You're on, big man,' he said. 'Now, do one.'

Logan pushed his jaw forwards, but he didn't say anything. He flicked his head, gesturing for his mates to follow. They all rode away, laughing.

Seth looked at his dad and put his hand over his face in despair. 'What have you done?'

BOYS IN THE BUSHES

The feeling of dread still lingered for Seth days later as the boys headed out of school after the final bell.

'Fancy coming back to mine?' he asked the others. 'We could have a session on *FIFA*?'

'Sounds good to me,' said Beefy.

Angelo was staring ahead.

Seth nudged him.

'Ange, what you reckon? Fancy some *FIFA*?'

Angelo just carried on staring.

Seth gave him a push this time. 'Ange?'

'The school team's practising tonight, aren't they?' said Angelo. 'Over there.'

'So?'

'So,' said Angelo, glancing around as other kids barged past. 'Why don't we spy on them?'

'What you on about?' asked Seth. 'Spy on them how? And why?'

'Get some inside info for The Big Game,' said

Angelo. 'See if we can spot any weaknesses and that?'

'You being serious?' asked Beefy.

'Yeah, man,' said Angelo. 'Think about it. Why have United got all those trees around The Park? It's to stop other teams spying on them.'

Beefy frowned. 'Is it? I thought it was just 'cos it looked nice.'

'I'm right, innit, Seth?' asked Angelo.

Seth shrugged. 'Makes sense, I guess.'

'See. It makes sense.'

'First time ever for you,' said Beefy.

'Shut it,' said Angelo. He gave Beefy a dig in the arm.

Beefy shrugged him off. Then he grabbed Angelo around the neck and took him in a headlock. He started rubbing his knuckles on Angelo's head.

'Oh yeah, you two will make great spies!' said Seth. He grabbed Beefy's arm and forced it off Angelo.

Angelo went to grab Beefy in retaliation, but Seth pushed him back.

'I think Ange might be on to something,' said Seth.

Angelo stopped. 'You do?'

'You do?' repeated Beefy.

'Won't hurt to have a look, will it?'

BOYS IN THE BUSHES

*   *   *

They made their way round to the school playing fields.

Every time Seth saw the field it reminded him of the try-outs. He still felt gutted about it all. He wondered whether he'd ever be able to see the pitch and not feel like that.

'Where we gonna stand?' asked Beefy. 'We don't want them to see us.'

'We could hide over there,' said Angelo. He was pointing at the row of bushes between the edge of the playing fields and the surrounding fencing. 'We'll be close enough to do some good spying and they won't see us. It'll be perfect.'

Seth pulled a face, unsure of the brilliance of the plan, but Angelo was already making his way over. One look at Beefy and they both followed.

They crossed the playing fields and began working their way into the bushes. It wasn't easy; they had the odd nasty thorn and stubby-ended branches which seemed designed to pull at coats and hair. These weren't bushes you were supposed to hide in.

'Crap idea, Ange,' Seth huffed, as he struggled to pull his bag out of sight. But Angelo was busy trying to extricate one of his cornrows from a thorn, cursing.

Eventually they felt well hidden among the foliage and crouched down. It was a good position, about thirty metres from one of the goal lines.

'I've always wanted to be a spy,' said Angelo.

'I thought you wanted to be a rapper?' Seth asked him. 'Or a footballer?'

'I can do all those things,' Angelo replied. 'I could be the world's first footballer slash rapper slash spy.'

'Slash loser, ' said Seth.

Beefy sniggered, while Angelo considered a devastating response.

'You're a loser,' he said.

'Shush,' said Beefy. 'They're coming.'

Across the field, the school team were making their way onto a nearby pitch. They were wearing the proper school strip – shirts with blue-and-white stripes, blue shorts, white socks. As much as Seth didn't want to admit it, they looked the business. He wished he was out there with them, instead of hiding in a stupid thorny bush.

Then there was a loud fart noise.

Followed by a horrible smell.

Seth and Angelo covered their faces.

'Sorry,' said Beefy. 'It's all this salad I'm eating.'

'Smells like you've been eating crap,' said Angelo.

'I haven't,' said Beefy. 'I've been really good.'

'I meant ACTUAL crap!' said Angelo.

'It's not that bad,' said Beefy. He wafted air towards his face and inhaled. 'Actually, that is pretty bad.' He covered his face too.

Seth and Angelo stifled bursts of laughter.

Beefy was right. It was pretty bad. Easily an eight on the stink-o-meter.

Out on the pitch, Steele was in his usual extra-tight black shorts. He sorted the players into two teams.

'I swear, mate,' said Angelo. 'You should've let Big Steve kung fu his face off.'

Beefy nodded.

Seth still found it hard to look at the PE teacher without feeling a simmering rage. He wondered what would've happened if his dad had come down to the school. It might've been one of the coolest things ever. He might've been a hero. He couldn't imagine there would've been many kids at the school who liked Steele. Or teachers for that matter. Or anyone. Anywhere. Ever. He was a Class A git. Still, it was best to keep out of real trouble.

Seth expected the players to be buzzing. They were playing for the school team. He'd have been well up for it. But the lads out on the pitch didn't look like they were buzzing. They didn't look anywhere near happy as Steele blew the whistle and the game started. The first minute or two's play was tentative, and most of them had their heads down.

Seth searched the pitch for Daniel Logan. He was easy to spot with his perfect floppy hair and girly face.

'COME ON!' bellowed Steele. 'AT LEAST BLOODY TRY!'

Steele was like one of those horrible drill sergeants you get in films; the miserable, mean dudes. They usually had bald heads and scary, bully-boy faces too. It was no surprise that none of the players looked happy with him as their coach.

'They don't look like they're having much fun, do they?' said Beefy.

'Nope,' Seth replied. 'Bet you still wish you'd got in though.'

'Who needs that lot?' said Angelo. 'We've got Freaks United. We're going to kick their butts!'

'You reckon?' asked Seth.

Angelo nodded. 'We will. Trust me.' He pulled his phone out of his pocket and pointed it towards the pitch.

'What you doing?' asked Beefy.

'I'm filming,' said Angelo. 'It's what spies do.'
'Is it?'

'Yeah, man. We can take it back. Look at it on the computer. Analyse it and that.'

'Like on *Match of the Day*?' asked Beefy.

'Exactly.'

'Have you heard yourselves?' asked Seth. 'Who do you think you are? Lineker and Shearer?'

Angelo shrugged.

'I think it's a good idea,' said Beefy.

Just then, Logan had a crack at goal.

The ball sailed just wide of the post and came thundering towards the bushes. There was no way it was going to stop in time.

'Oh no,' whispered Seth.

The ball rolled on at a pace into the bush. It stopped right in front of them, jammed under a spiny branch.

Seth looked down at the ball. Then up at Angelo and Beefy. He blinked and swallowed.

Logan jogged over.

'Be quiet,' whispered Seth. 'Don't even breathe.'

Logan stopped by the bushes. He peered in, looking for the ball.

Seth turned to Beefy and Angelo.

Angelo's cheeks were inflated and Beefy's face was all screwed up. He looked like he was in pain.

Seth flicked his head to ask Beefy what was the matter.

Beefy shook his head.

Then there was another loud fart noise.

Logan stared into the bush. His eyes met Seth's. He blinked. Frowned.

Seth's heart sank.

'What you doing?' asked Logan. Then he covered his face. 'And what's that smell?'

'Sorry,' said Beefy.

Seth handed the ball to Logan. Then he covered his face too.

'COME ON!' shouted Steele from over on the pitch. 'WE HAVEN'T GOT ALL DAY.'

'THERE'S SOME LADS IN THE BUSHES, SIR!' called Logan.

'YOU WHAT?' shouted Steele.

Steele stomped over and peered in at Seth and his mates.

'What you doing in there?' he demanded. Then he pulled away. 'And what's that awful stink?'

'We're... erm... doing some science stuff,' said Seth.

'Yeah right,' said Logan. 'You're spying on us.'

Steele straightened up and put his hands on his hips. 'Spying?'

'We're playing them,' said Logan. 'Our team

against theirs. If that's what you can even call it!'

Steele turned to the huddle in the bushes. 'That right?' he asked. 'You lot spying?'

Seth shook his head. 'No, sir. Just science stuff.'

'Whatever it is you're doing, I don't want you doing it in my bloody bush!' said Steele. 'Now go on, clear off!'

Seth, Angelo and Beefy fought their way out of the hedge under the PE teacher's watchful gaze.

As they trudged away across the field Logan shouted after them, 'WE'LL BE SEEING YOU, FREAKS!'

Seth looked back. All the players were watching them, laughing.

'That didn't go very well, did it?' said Seth. 'We look like Class A donkeys.'

'Maybe not,' said Angelo. 'At least Logan got a mouthful of Beefy's fart!'

GIRLS AGAINST BOYS

Beefy and Angelo called round later that evening for training.

'What's Big Steve got planned for tonight?' asked Angelo, as Seth let them in. 'More punching and stuff? I wouldn't mind some more punching.'

Seth shook his head. 'You worry me, you know that?'

'Evening, lads,' said Steve. He was standing in the living room doorway wearing shorts and a black United away shirt from ten seasons previous. It was one of his favourites. It had 'Hart' on the back and a number nine. 'I was thinking we could try something different tonight. Take it up a notch.'

'What you on about?' asked Seth. 'Up a notch?'

Steve drove them in his car. Seth in the passenger seat, Angelo and Beefy in the back.

After a short drive Steve turned into a massive car park next to a gym. It was a huge building with lots of windows.

'Are we going in there, Stevie?' asked Angelo. 'We gonna pump some iron?' He flexed his arm and gave his puny bicep a squeeze. 'I reckon I could press about seventy kilos.'

'That right?' asked Steve.

'Yeah. Is that a lot?'

'It's a fair bit,' said Steve.

'You couldn't lift seventy feathers,' said Beefy.

'Bet you could,' said Angelo. 'Bet you could lift loads, with all the sweets you stuff into your face. Your arm's always going.'

'All right, lads, that's enough,' said Steve.

The boys followed Steve out of the car and into the building next to the gym – The Soccer Dome. Seth had been here loads of times. It was where his dad played five-a-side.

Steve joked with the girl at reception and gave her some money. 'Come on, lads,' he said. The boys followed him down a corridor.

Steve pushed open a set of double doors and led the boys out onto an indoor five-a-side pitch. The lights were really bright overhead and their trainers squeaked on the shiny, wooden floor.

'Nice one,' said Angelo. 'Are we gonna practise in here tonight?'

'More than practise,' said Steve. 'You're gonna play a match.'

Seth felt himself growing suddenly hot and slightly nervous. 'A match?' he asked. 'Against who?'

'Against that lot,' Steve pointed over to the corner of the room.

There were a small group of girls gathered together.

Seth recognised one instantly. Alan's sister. Laura.

There were four other girls. The goalie was as big as Beefy. Her ginger hair was pulled back with an Alice band. There was a tall, skinny girl with blonde, curly hair. A short girl with short hair and pointed ears who looked a bit like a pixie. The last girl was chubby with plaited hair. She looked more like a boy – apart from the plaits. They each had the same football shirt on. It was black and it said 'JP Windows' on the front. Seth didn't fancy any of these girls. Apart from Laura. In fact, he wasn't entirely sure the others were even girls at all. Especially the chubby one.

The doors opened and Alan bounded in. He was wearing a T-shirt with Bart Simpson on it. Bart was saying, 'Don't have a cow, man!'

Seth couldn't help smiling. He was starting to

like Alan's stupid T-shirts.

'Hello, Mr Hart,' said Alan. 'Hello everyone else.'

'Just "Steve",' said Seth's dad.

'Oh, yeah,' said Alan. 'I mean Just Steve.' He grinned.

'Alan's helped me arrange this, haven't you?' said Steve.

'Yeah,' said Alan. 'I thought it would be good. With you lot fancying my sister and that.'

Seth felt his face go hot. 'Who said we fancied her?' he asked.

'They did,' said Alan. He pointed at Angelo and Beefy.

'Yeah,' said Angelo. 'We do.'

'You might,' said Seth.

'You don't?' asked Beefy.

'I didn't say that,' said Seth.

'See,' said Angelo.

'So, you've all got your eyes on the girl then?' asked Steve.

'No,' said Seth.

'We have,' said Angelo.

'Just as long as it doesn't get in the way of your game.' Steve gave the lads a wink.

Seth sort of smiled.

'So we're really playing girls?' asked Beefy.

'Yep,' Steve confirmed.

'Are they *all* girls?' asked Seth.

'I think so,' said his dad. 'They're all girls, aren't they, Big Al?'

'Big Al'? thought Seth. Since when was Alan 'Big Al'?

'They are,' said Alan. 'Even the fat one. I know she doesn't look like a girl, but she is. I saw her bra once when she was around at my house. It was pink.'

Seth and the others cracked up laughing.

'Come on, Stevie,' said Angelo. 'Girls can't play football. Everyone knows that.' He looked around at his mates with a grin.

'Well you'll have no problem beating them then, will you?' said Steve. 'I'll go in goal. You lot figure out where you're gonna play.'

Steve went over to the girls.

'Is this a joke?' asked Beefy.

'I dunno,' said Seth. 'Is it a joke, Alan?'

Alan grinned. He shook his head.

'Is your sister any good?' asked Angelo.

Alan grinned. He shook his head.

Seth sighed. 'Whatever, let's just play, yeah? Me and Beefy will stay back. Angelo, you go midfield. Alan, you go up front. I'll try and bounce the ball off you into the goal.'

'You mean I might score?' asked Alan.

Seth looked around at the others. 'I wouldn't

get your hopes up.'

'Oh,' said Alan.

'But try,' said Angelo.

'Yeah,' added Seth. 'You can try.'

Alan looked pleased. 'I will,' he said. 'I'll really try!'

The boys jogged into their positions as Steve headed over to their half. 'Right, boys,' he said. 'Now remember, complacency can be a killer.'

'Complay-what?' asked Angelo.

'Don't underestimate them,' Steve continued. 'Show them some respect.' He walked off and took his place in goal.

'Respect?' said Angelo. 'How about we give their butts a proper kicking instead!'

Seth and Beefy sniggered.

The girls took their positions.

Laura bounced the ball on the wooden floor. Her long dark hair was tied back. Her big brown eyes sparkled under the bright lights in the gym. She looked awesome in a football shirt. A full-blown ten on the fit-o-meter.

'You want to kick off?' she asked.

Seth stared at her some more.

'Hello?' asked Laura. 'Anyone home.'

'Yeah, sorry, whatever you, err, think's best.'

Beefy and Angelo sniggered.

Laura raised her eyebrows a little. She put

the ball down and knocked it back to Chubby.

Chubby knocked it to Pixie.

Alan went after her, but she took the ball past him with ease.

That was nothing unexpected, thought Seth. A small child would take the ball past Alan Block with ease.

Pixie laid the ball off to Laura.

She went one way, took the ball the other, leaving Angelo as twisted as his cornrows.

Seth pulled his head back in shock. Now he was backtracking towards his own goal.

'I've got her,' said Beefy. He charged at Laura.

She popped the ball between his legs. 'Megsed!' shouted Laura. She was around him with the ball under her control.

There was a loud THUD.

The whole room shook.

Beefy was on his backside.

Now Laura was charging at Seth.

Seth did as he'd always been taught. He kept his eyes on the ball. It was tough though. Laura was pulling out step-over after step-over like she was Christiano Ronaldo.

Seth finally chose his moment to lunge in with a tackle.

Laura pulled a Zidane pirouette out of nowhere, leaving Seth in a knot.

Seth could only watch as she blasted the ball into the bottom corner.

Laura punched the air as the other girls cheered and congratulated her.

'That's how girls do it,' she said, as she walked past Seth. She tousled his hair.

Seth blinked a few times and looked around at his team-mates.

Beefy and Angelo's mouths were hanging open.

'She's like... Messi,' said Angelo.

'She's not,' said Alan. 'She's really tidy. You should see her room.'

Seth stopped counting after the girls' fifteenth goal. It was embarrassing. Actually, it was beyond embarrassing. It was humiliating. The Freaks couldn't even get close to the girls. Chubby was pulling the strings in midfield. Pixie was solid at the back. Tall Girl had tekkers. And then there was Laura. Laura Laura Laura. She was scoring from every angle. Volleys. Placed shots. Curlers. She was a gorgeous goal-scoring machine. It wasn't fair.

Seth was really grateful when his dad called an end to the game. Not only had they been humiliated, but they'd been humiliated by girls. And worst of all, one of those girls was a girl

Seth fancied.

'Gather round, boys,' said Steve.

The boys collapsed in heaps on the wooden floor.

Beefy was sweating so much that Seth thought he might drown.

'So what did you learn from that?'

'We're crap,' said Angelo.

'No,' said Steve. 'You're not.'

'Girls can play football,' said Beefy.

'Yep. Anything else?'

'These floors make really nice squeaky sounds,' said Alan. He kicked his feet against the floor, making a really nice squeaky sound.

'More important than that, Big Al,' said Steve

'Why'd you keep calling him "Big Al"?' Seth asked.

'Just a name,' Steve replied. 'You like it, don't you, Big Al?'

'I do, Steve.' He grinned. 'Does it suit me?'

'Jesus,' said Seth.

'Go on then, Seth,' Steve said. 'What did you learn?'

'We shouldn't underestimate our opposition,' said Seth.

'Ding ding! Right answer. Never underestimate your opponent.'

'Do you think Logan's lot will underestimate

us?' asked Seth.

'Probably,' said Steve. 'But we can use that to our advantage.'

'You know what else might help us,' Beefy piped up. 'If we had Laura playing for us.'

The boys looked around at each other and nodded.

'Do you think she would?' Seth asked Alan.

'Maybe,' he replied. 'You should go and ask her.'

Seth looked over at Laura. Not only was she pretty, but she was also better than him at football. Seth didn't think he could be more intimidated by a girl if he wanted to be. He was at a solid eight on the suck-o-meter. 'Why don't we all go?' he suggested.

The boys looked around at each other.

Then slowly they all picked themselves up off the floor.

Seth led the boys over to Laura as she said goodbye to Pixie. He stood there for a moment, trying to work out what he should say.

Laura was crouched down. She pulled off her trainers and pulled on big chunky Dr. Martin boots. They had a red flower on them. They were cool. She looked up at Seth. 'So you're Freaks, are you?' she asked.

Seth blinked.

'That's what you're called isn't it?'

Seth blinked again.

'Do you talk?'

'Erm, yeah,' Seth said.

'You don't look like freaks,' said Laura.

'I... erm... it's just our name,' Seth replied.

'I wanted Ninjas,' said Angelo. 'But they didn't like it.'

Laura smiled.

'We were thinking,' said Seth. 'We've got this match against this idiot, Daniel Logan, and his team in a few weeks and... well...'

'You want me to play for you?' asked Laura.

'Would you?'

'I don't know,' she shrugged.

Seth felt his heart sink a little.

'Go on, sis,' said Alan. 'I don't like Daniel.'

'And do you like this lot?' she asked.

Alan nodded quickly. 'They're my best friends!'

Seth didn't know whether to smile or feel a bit scared.

'OK,' said Laura. 'I'll play for you.'

'Get in!' said Beefy.

Angelo followed up with a 'Woohoo!'

Seth smiled at Alan. He could've kissed the little weirdo.

'One condition,' Laura added.

'Name it,' said Seth.

'You get the other players,' she told him. 'I'm not helping with any of that.'

'From where?' asked Seth.

'That's up to you.' Laura stood up, hauled her backpack over her shoulder and walked away.

Seth looked around at his mates. 'Where are we going to find six more players?'

TOP SECRET BUSINESS

After training, the boys headed back to Seth's house. Even Alan was invited this time. They kicked off their trainers and went up into his room.

Seth sat in his swivel chair and everyone else plopped themselves down on his bed.

'Wow,' said Alan. 'Cool room.'

'Thanks,' Seth replied.

'What are all these little things?' asked Alan. He pulled the duvet cover up, pointing at the repeat pattern of the United crest to Seth.

'That's United's badge,' Seth told him. 'Every club has a badge. You know who United are, right?'

Alan grinned. 'Freaks United?' he asked.

'Nah, man,' said Angelo. 'The proper United. The town's football team.'

'And the best team in the world!' Beefy added.

Alan shrugged.

'Do you live in a cave?' Seth asked him.

Alan grinned. 'I wish! I'd like to be a bat. Or a cat. Or a...'

'We get it. You're weird.' Seth shook his head. He pulled the notepad and felt tips out of his drawer.

'Are we having a team meeting?' asked Angelo.

'Yep,' said Seth.

'This is exciting,' said Alan. 'I've never been to a team meeting before. What happens?'

'We're not really sure,' said Beefy. 'What happens again?'

Seth looked thoughtful. 'I reckon we need to make a list,' he said. 'Of potential targets.'

'We're not going to assassinate people, are we?' asked Alan. 'It's just... I don't like blood. It makes me go all funny inside.'

Beefy and Angelo looked at each other.

'We're not going to assassinate anyone,' said Seth. 'I meant a list of lads who might want to play for us. Anyone got any ideas?'

'What about that Sam kid?' said Beefy. 'He was pretty good.'

'Yeah,' said Seth. 'What would you rate him out of ten?'

'For what?' asked Angelo.

'For tekkers and that?' said Seth.

'Dunno,' said Beefy. 'Seven?'

'Eight?' said Angelo.

'NINE!' shouted Alan.

'Nine?' asked Seth. 'Really?'

'Yeah,' said Alan. 'Did I win?'

'It's not a game, you muppet,' said Angelo.

'Right, I'll give him an eight,' said Seth. 'Do you think he has any special skills we can use?'

'Like computer hacking?' asked Alan.

'I meant football skills,' said Seth.

'Put 'mad skills',' said Angelo.

'What?' asked Seth.

'Put 'mad skills' on your list,' said Angelo.

'Whatever,' said Seth. He wrote 'mad skills' on the page.

'Strength?' said Beefy.

'He's good at passing too,' said Angelo.

'Where'd you reckon we might find him?' asked Seth.

'At school?' said Beefy.

'Outside of school?' asked Seth.

'Why does that matter?' asked Angelo.

'Because we want to keep this undercover,' said Seth. 'We don't want Logan or Steele knowing about our plans. Logan already knows we were spying on them. He probably thinks we won't be able to get a team together. I want it to be a surprise. You with me?'

Angelo and Beefy smiled and nodded at each

other.

'Top secret business,' said Angelo. 'I like it.'

'Like spies?' asked Alan.

'Exactly,' said Angelo.

Alan grinned. 'I've always wanted to be a spy.'

'Me too!' said Angelo.

'I look a bit like James Bond, don't you think?' said Alan. He put his hands together and made his fingers into a gun. He pointed it at Seth. 'The name's Block. Alan Block.'

'Are you mental?' asked Seth.

Beefy and Angelo creased.

Alan started laughing too.

Once they all calmed down, Seth got them back to business. 'Come on, then. Where'd you think we might find him?'

'In his house?' said Beefy.

'Brilliant input there, Beef,' said Seth.

'What? You WOULD find him in his house.'

'And where does he live?' asked Seth.

'We could follow him,' Alan suggested.

'Bit creepy,' said Seth. 'But we could, I guess. I don't think there's any other choice. OK, tomorrow, after school, we'll follow him. Do you think he'll join the team?'

'Maybe,' said Beefy. 'He obviously likes football.'

Seth nodded. He made more notes on his pad.

'What about that really tall boy?' said Alan. 'He might be good.'

'Yeah, that boy in our year,' said Beefy. 'He's about ten feet tall!'

'I saw him in the library,' said Alan. 'Last Saturday. I was in there getting some books out about cats.'

'OK,' said Seth, ignoring Alan's comment about books and cats. 'But can he play?'

'Who cares,' said Beefy. 'Just kick the ball up to him and let the ball bounce off his head!'

'What would you give him for tekkers, Angelo?' asked Seth.

'I'd say four.'

'Five,' said Beefy.

'NINE!' shouted Alan. 'Did I win this time?'

Seth shook his head.

'What about that Ryo kid?' said Beefy. 'He could play.'

'And that Curtis,' said Angelo. 'That little guy. He's the fastest I've ever seen.'

'Really?' said Seth.

'Yeah, man,' said Angelo. 'I've seen him running away from some lads. He was like Usain Bolt!'

They were cooking on gas now. That was something his dad said when things suddenly started to work out.

'What about Alex?' said Alan.

'Alex who?'

'I don't know his second name. But he's scary-looking.'

'You mean that goth kid?' said Beefy.

'Yeah,' said Angelo. 'He's proper scary. No one would go near him!'

'Nice,' said Seth. 'Good job, Alan.'

'Yeah,' said Angelo. He held his first out to Alan.

Alan bumped it. 'Could you call me "Big Al"?' he asked.

'Serious?' said Seth.

Alan nodded.

The boys sat and came up with ideas until Seth had a list of five players and their details written in red felt tip. It started off really neatly and then got a bit ragged towards the end, but Seth was pleased with their work.

LIST OF POTENTIAL TARGETS

Name: Sam Wall
Tekkers: 8/10
Mad skills: Solid, strong, good at passing
Position: defence
Where to find: follow him from school

(not in a creepy way)
Will he join? Good chance

Name: Tall Boy
Tekkers: 5/10
Mad skills: Tall-ness
Position: up front
Where to find: library
Will he join? 5/10

Name: Ryo Something
Tekkers: 8/10
Mad skills: fast/good at tackling
Position: defence
Where to find: follow him home from school
    (not in a creepy way)
Will he join? 8/10

Name: Little Curtis
Tekkers: 4/10
Mad skills: fast/wears glasses
    (Alan thinks that's cool)
Position: wing
Where to find: laboratory
    (Alan and Angelo's suggestion)
Will he join? 5/10

Name: Scary Alex

Tekkers: 2/10
Mad skills: scary goth face
Position: defence
Where to find: Goth Green where all the goths live
Will he join? 2/10

'Good work, lads,' said Seth. 'But we still need one more. Any ideas?'

They each looked around at one another.

Seth had an idea. He wondered whether it was an idea they were all having. He was pretty sure it was on Angelo and Beefy's minds. He didn't know what was on Alan's mind. Talking cats. Dancing pigs. Who knew what went on up in there?

'There is one more person,' said Seth.

'Who?' asked Beefy.

'Jordan.'

'Jordan McGrath?' asked Angelo.

'He can play,' said Seth.

'He can probably stab you in the face too!' said Beefy.

Angelo sniggered. Then he stopped. 'Beef's right,' he said. 'He probably could stab you in the face.'

'I don't like the sound of stabbing,' said Alan. 'Especially not in the face.'

'Don't worry, Alan,' Seth reassured him. 'No

one's gonna get stabbed in the face.'

Alan put his hand on Seth's. 'Thank you,' he said.

Seth shrugged Alan's hand away and grimaced. 'But we could ask him,' said Seth. 'What's he *really* gonna do?'

'Errr, stab you?' said Beefy. 'In the face? Did you not hear me mention the stabbing and the faces?'

'He won't stab us,' said Seth. 'D'you really think he would?'

He looked around at the others. No one said anything.

THE TALL BOY

The next day, after school, Seth met up with the others outside the main entrance.

'So we up for this?' he asked

'I am,' said Alan. He unzipped his bag and began pulling things out. He handed Seth a fake moustache and beard. Angelo was given a deerstalker and a pipe. Then Alan passed Beefy some glow-in-the-dark fangs and a messy brown werewolf wig.

'What's this?' asked Seth.

'Your disguises,' Alan replied, with a look of satisfaction.

'This?' asked Seth. 'Really?'

'Good thinking, Big Al,' said Angelo.

Beefy looked impressed. 'Yeah,' he said. 'Nice one!'

'Thanks!' said Alan. He took out a balaclava and pulled it over his own head.

'You guys think this is a good idea?' asked

Seth.

'Spies have to have disguises,' said Angelo.

'It's the rules,' Beefy added. He stuck his fake teeth in his mouth. He pulled his wig on. Then he nudged Seth. 'There'sh Sham,' he said.

'Thanksh!' said Seth, spotting the big lad ahead of them.

Angelo and Alan laughed.

The four of them put on their disguises and began following Sam through the crowds of other kids. Seth counted the funny looks they were getting from the other kids. Three. Seven. Nine. He stopped after ten.

'Do you really need to wear these things?' Seth asked Angelo, who was next to him.

'Come on, man,' his mate replied. 'Stop being such a girl.' He sucked on his pretend pipe. Angelo didn't seem to care and somehow, neither did Seth.

The boys followed Sam out of the school gates, down the street and towards the shopping precinct. They made sure they kept about twenty or so metres back, in case he spotted them.

'Can we not just go up to him?' asked Beefy. 'I mean, we're out of school now.'

Seth thought about it. He realised there were a few holes in his plan. In fact, he was hardly sure whether what they had could be called a plan at all. 'OK, yeah,' he said. 'Come on.'

They quickened their pace. They passed the pet shop, the DIY store, the Bargain Basement. Then Sam headed into the fruit-and-veg shop.

The boys stopped outside, watching through the window.

Sam was talking to a man who looked about sixty. He had on one of those flat caps and his cheeks were rosy, as though he'd been out in the snow. He handed Sam an apron as Sam joined him behind the counter.

'Shall we go in?' Deefy suggested.

'Yeah, come on,' said Seth. He held the shop door open and flicked his head, so the rest of them followed him into the shop.

'You all right there fellas?' asked the man. 'Not Halloween already, is it?'

Seth had almost forgotten the stupid disguises. He took off his fake moustache and glasses and looked around at his mates, expecting them to do the same.

They didn't.

'You can take the disguises off now,' said Seth.

Alan groaned. Angelo too. But they all took off their disguises.

'You're not here to rob the place, are you?' asked the man.

'No, no,' said Seth. 'We... we just came to see

Sam.'

'Me?' asked Sam. He frowned. His biceps were twice the size of Seth's. He had a bottom lip that seemed slightly too big for his mouth and the same red cheeks as the greengrocer behind the counter.

'Yeah,' said Seth. 'We go to your school.'

Sam nodded.

'We were wondering...'

'Do you want to be a Freak?' asked Alan. He spat the words out quickly. It was as though he couldn't keep them inside him.

'What they on about, Sam?' asked the man. 'A freak? Are you some kind of weird band?'

'Yeah?' said Sam. 'What you on about?'

'We're starting a football team,' Seth told him. 'We wondered whether you wanted to play for us?'

Sam looked at the greengrocer. Then he looked at Seth. 'Just you lot?' he asked.

'So far,' said Seth.

'We've got a list though,' said Angelo. 'You were top!'

'Top of the list,' said the greengrocer. 'That's not bad, is it?'

'So do you want to play?' asked Seth.

'What's in it for us?' asked the greengrocer.

'What do you mean?' Seth turned to him.

'Well, I'm Sam's agent,' said the greengrocer. 'What's in it for us?' He winked at Sam.

'We could cook your favourite tea?' suggested Alan.

'Or,' said the greengrocer. 'You could meet us on Sunday over on the allotments near your school. I've got a delivery you can help with.'

Seth looked around at his mates. 'A delivery of what?' he asked.

'It'll be a surprise,' said the greengrocer. 'Something you can all get stuck into.'

Seth looked around at his mates.

They nodded.

'OK,' said Seth.

'Never miss a trick, do you, Grandad?' Sam said.

'You know me,' said Sam's grandad. He winked at the boys now.

Seth watched as Alan tried to wink back. It looked more like he was sucking on one of Beefy's Haribo Sours. Seth smirked.

They all left the shop.

Outside, Seth pulled his list and pen out of his pocket. He put a big tick next to Sam's name.

'One down, five more to go,' he said.

Alan held his hand out, palms down.

'What you doing?' asked Beefy.

'We should all put our hands in,' said Alan.

'Like they do in the films.'

'No,' said Seth. 'We shouldn't.' He swatted Alan's hand away.

The following Saturday Seth, Beefy and Angelo were standing outside the library in the middle of town. It was a nice, sunny day and it felt really warm; T-shirt weather, Steve called it.

Seth had his list again and they had a plan for the day. Sort of. Library first for Tall Boy. Then on to Games Workshop where they hoped they might find Little Curtis. Beefy had eavesdropped on a conversation at school and heard Curtis talking about it with a mate. After that, it was on to Goth Green to find Scary Alex. Ryo, they still weren't sure on. They'd agreed to leave Jordan for a little while. They needed to build up to him. Save the scariest for last.

Seth had put his favourite shirt on. It was chequered, green and black. All the lads looked smart. Seth had told them to dress to impress. He was serious about this team and he wanted the other kids they approached to take them seriously too. Beefy had a shirt on too. It was light blue. Angelo was wearing what looked like a brand-new Nike hoodie.

Seth looked at his watch. It was just after ten. They were still waiting for Alan.

'Can I tell you guys something?' said Beefy. The other two nodded.

'I went on Alan's website last night.'

'What's on there?' asked Angelo. 'Is there loads of stuff about dead bodies?'

'No. There's a talking cat.'

'You what?' said Seth.

'His cat says "oh my god",' said Beefy.

'No it doesn't,' said Angelo.

'That's what it sounds like,' said Beefy. 'Oh my god. Oh my god. Oh my god. There's just loads of videos of his cat saying 'oh my god'. They've got millions of views!'

'No way,' said Seth.

'Serious,' said Beefy. 'Have a look when you get home!'

Alan appeared from around the corner. He was wearing a sheepskin coat and a flat-cap. He looked like one of the old-style football managers Seth had seen in some of his dad's ancient books.

'All right.' Alan nodded at the boys.

Seth looked at his mates. Then at Alan. 'Alan?' he asked. 'Why are you dressed like Del Boy?'

'I thought I'd dress like a football manager,' said Alan. 'If we're going to ask people to play for us, we want them to think we're professional. You said it. That reminds me!' Alan stuck his hand in his pocket. He pulled out a stack of business cards and handed a pile each to Seth, Beefy and Angelo.

Seth looked at the card. It said:

Name: Seth Hart
Twitter: @Sethiscool
Website: www.ilovesethhart.com
Skills: playing football, being nice,
being cool, being funny

'Erm, thanks, Alan,' said Seth. 'But I don't have a website. Or a Twitter.'

Angelo stared at his own card. 'Me neither.'

'Same here,' said Beefy.

'You do now,' said Alan. 'You all do!'

'That's a bit creepy,' said Beefy.

Seth smiled. Alan was indeed a bit creepy. But he was starting to like him. If Seth's dad was going to describe Alan, he'd say something like, 'He doesn't have a bad bone in his body.'

Seth stared in through the glass doors of the library before pushing them open and ushering the boys inside.

They wandered through the huge high-ceilinged room to an area where there were several desks and a couple of rows of PCs.

Alan grabbed Seth's shoulder. 'There's Tall Boy!' He pointed over to a kid who was sitting at a desk writing in an exercise book. He had big sticky-out ears and big sticky-out teeth. Everything about him was big and sticky-out, pretty much. Apart from his jeans. They were tight around his skinny legs and too short. Seth figured that most jeans were probably too short for Tall Boy.

'What's he doing?' asked Angelo.

'Homework probably,' said Alan.

'Homework on a Saturday?' asked Angelo. 'Now THAT is a freak!'

The others laughed.

Tall Boy stood up. He must've been six foot five. He was taller than Seth's dad. He was taller than Seth on his dad's shoulders. OK, maybe not quite. But he wasn't far off.

'So?' asked Seth. 'What does everyone think? Shall we go and poach him?'

'Like an egg!' said Alan.

'Come on,' said Seth. 'Let's do it.' He strode over to Tall Boy, who was back in his chair, writing.

'Hi,' said Seth.

Tall Boy looked up at Seth and the rest of them.

'I'm Seth. And this is Beefy, Angelo and Alan.'

'Big Al,' said Alan.

'I meant Big Al,' said Seth.

'I'm John,' said Tall Boy. 'Nice to meet you all. But I can't help you with your homework. I've got to do this. Maybe next week?'

'I'm not here about homework,' Seth told him. 'I'm here about football.'

'Football?' John looked puzzled. 'I don't know much about football.'

'That's cool,' said Angelo. 'I don't know much about homework.'

'We want you to play for us,' Seth told him. 'We want you to be a Freak.'

'A Freak?'

'That's what our team's called,' said Beefy. 'Freaks United.'

'I wanted Ninjas FC, but they wouldn't let me,' said Angelo.

'You want me to play for a football team? But I can't play football,' said John.

'Neither can I,' said Alan. 'Here.' He handed John one of his business cards and tipped his hat to him.

John studied the card and frowned. 'But I've got so much school work to do. My parents won't let me play football.'

'They don't need to know,' said Angelo.

'You can tell them you're doing extra study or something,' Beefy put in.

John's eyes widened. 'Do you think?' he asked.

He seemed chuffed that they were talking to him.

'Course,' said Seth.

John screwed his face up. 'It might be fun,' he said.

'It'll definitely be fun.'

'Definitely?'

Seth thought about some of his dad's training sessions. 'Mostly,' he said.

John looked up at Seth for a moment. His eyes flicked to Beefy. Then to Angelo, who grinned. Then to Alan, who put his hands together as though he was praying. 'You really want me to play?' he asked. 'You sure?'

'That's why we're here,' said Seth.

John took a breath. 'OK,' he said. 'I'll join.'

'Sweet,' said Seth.

'On one condition,' said John.

'What condition?'

'You join my homework group,' John said.

'What homework group?' asked Beefy.

'The one I'm starting,' said John. 'Right now.'

'Right now?' asked Angelo.

'Right now,' said John. 'And every Saturday from now on.'

Seth groaned. He looked around at his friends. None of them looked happy. Even Alan looked distressed. 'Give me a moment,' said Seth. He took his friends into a huddle.

'So?' asked Seth. 'What do you think?'

'I don't like the sound of homework group,' said Angelo. 'Homework group sounds crap.'

'Yeah, I know,' said Seth. 'But we need players, don't we?'

'I'll do it,' said Alan. 'Even though I don't want to. For the Freaks.'

Seth grinned. 'Good man, Big Al.'

Beefy sighed. 'Go on then.'

Seth looked at Angelo. 'Just you, Ange.'

'Do I have to?'

'Come on,' said Seth. 'For the Freaks.'

'The Freaks,' repeated Alan.

'Ahh, man,' Angelo sighed. 'For the Freaks then.'

Seth gave him a pat on the back. Then he turned around to John. 'OK, John, you've got yourself a deal.' He held his hand up for a high five.

John high-fived him. Then he high-fived the others.

Apart from Alan. Who tried, but missed.

'Don't suppose you might know where we'd find any of these guys?' asked Seth. He pulled his list out and showed it to John.

'I think Curtis hangs out at the Games Workshop on a Saturday,' he told them.

'Told you,' said Beefy.

'Can't help you with the others,' said John. 'Sorry.'

Once they'd given John the details of the next training session, they left the library. Outside, Seth put a tick next to Tall Boy. He also wrote John in brackets.

'Right!' Seth felt fired up now. Two down. 'On to Games Workshop!'

FIND MORE FREAKS!

Seth led the boys through the busy town centre. He looked around at the mums and dads and kids and old people as he passed. He wondered whether any of them were on a mission like him and his mates. He didn't know. What he did know was that it felt pretty exciting to be on a mission.

They reached Games Workshop and stopped outside. There was a cardboard cut-out of a horrible-looking little troll-thing in the window. It was green and grinning, wearing pants made of fur. It was picking its nose.

'I've heard about these places,' said Angelo. 'They do weird stuff to you in here, don't they? Like experiments and stuff?'

'No they don't,' said Seth, even though he wasn't sure. He had no idea what went on in Games Workshop.

Seth looked around and pushed the door

open. He'd never been inside before. He'd looked in often enough whenever he went past and it always seemed to be busy. But what exactly anyone was doing was beyond him. People seemed to go in there and stay there. Like all day. Some of them gathered around tables, probably chanting and making up spells. Maybe conjuring up demons and trolls. A full on ten on the weird-o-meter.

Inside the shop there were shelves filled with loads of these little figures and a huge table that had model castles and hills and armies built on it. Seth thought it looked kind of cool. Still a bit weird. But kind of cool.

'Ker-ching! There's Curtis,' said Beefy. He pointed over to a small kid with huge glasses. He was wearing a blue hoodie that was way too big for him, with a sort of horseshoe on it.

'*He's* really fast?' asked Seth.

'He's like Speedy Gonzales on steroids!' said Angelo.

There were a couple of other lads with Curtis. One was tall and skinny with a big nose. The other was short like Curtis. His hair looked wet and he had loads of freckles. They both had the same hoodies on as Curtis, like some geeky little gang.

Seth led the way over. 'Hi Curtis,' he said.

Curtis looked up from his little models. 'Errr, hello?'

Seth didn't waste any time. 'Do you fancy playing for a football team?'

Curtis screwed his face up. 'Not funny, guys,' he said. He looked past Seth and his mates and out through the window of the shop. 'Who's put you up to this?' he asked.

'No one,' said Seth.

'Come on,' said Curtis. 'This is a joke, isn't it?'

'We're being serious,' Seth told him. 'We've got a team...'

'Freaks United,' said Alan. 'But not actual freaks. Not with big feet or lots of arms or anything.' He grinned.

'But I don't know anything about football,' said Curtis.

'We know,' said Seth. 'But we've heard how fast you are. We thought you'd be perfect.'

'I don't think I'm interested,' said Curtis. 'Thanks for the offer though.'

'Go on,' said Beefy. 'It'll be fun.'

'We could do something for you too,' said Alan.

Seth felt like smashing his head into the nearest wall, but he didn't fancy having a warrior figure's little sword embedded in his forehead.

'What do you mean?'

'We're helping Sam tomorrow,' Alan told

Curtis. 'We've joined John's homework club. They're both going to join our team. We could do something for you too.'

Seth scowled at Alan.

Curtis looked around at his mates. Then he grinned. 'There might be something you could do,' he said.

'Here we go,' said Seth. 'What?'

'We've got a Warhammer tournament coming up,' said Curtis. 'And we could do with getting some practice in. You guys could play us?'

'But we don't know how to play any of this stuff,' said Seth. He went to pick up a little model of an elf with a sword, but Curtis slapped his hand away.

'I don't know how to play football,' said Curtis, and he grinned.

Seth sighed. 'So you want us to, what, come here?'

'After school,' said Curtis. 'Every day.'

'No way,' said Angelo. 'I'm not coming here every day!'

'Four times a week?' said Curtis.

Seth shrugged.

'Three?' said Curtis. 'OK, twice?'

'Erm...'

Curtis interrupted Seth before he could say anything. 'Just the once?'

'OK,' said Seth. He scratched his head.

'Yes!' said Curtis. Then he did a fist pump.

His friends patted him on the back.

Seth pulled out his list. 'Do you know where I might find this guy?' He pointed to Ryo's name.

'Sure,' said Curtis. 'I've been to his house for tea.'

'What did you have?' asked Beefy.

'Ignore him,' said Seth. 'Where does Ryo live?'

'Number three, Redtop Drive.'

'I know where that is,' said Alan. 'It's not far from my house.'

'Are you going there now?' asked Curtis.

Seth nodded.

'Be prepared,' said Curtis.

'Prepared for what?' asked Beefy.

'Just stuff,' said Curtis. He looked around at his friends and smirked.

Seth and the boys left the shop. Outside, Seth put a tick next to Curtis' name. 'Going well so far, boys,' he said.

'Going well?' asked Angelo. 'Every time we go to see someone, we end up having to do jobs or join stupid clubs!'

'You want your own team, you have to put the work in,' said Seth. 'Do you want your own team?'

'Yeah,' said Angelo, quietly. 'Whatever.'

'Well then,' said Seth. 'But we'll do our best to get out of this Warhammer thing, I promise.'

When they got off the bus, Alan led them all the way to Redtop Drive. It was a normal-looking street, just like Alan's, but Seth had an idea they were going to be in line for something weird after what Curtis had told them. Of course there was also the possibility that Curtis was winding them up. Curtis didn't look like a wind-up merchant though.

'This is the one,' said Alan.

There was no waiting at the bottom of the drive this time. Alan was marching right up to the door before Seth could even think about discussing tactics. Seth and the others followed after.

Alan rang the doorbell.

After a moment a woman answered the door. She had dark curly hair and a T-shirt that said 'Lanzarote' on it. 'Hello?' she said.

'Is Ryo in?' asked Seth.

'He's just in the garage,' she said. 'Why don't you go around?'

'Thanks,' said Seth.

They went around to the garage at the side of the house.

Seth paused outside the closed doors.

Music was playing from inside. It wasn't rap music or indie music or music from the charts. It sounded like music they played at a circus. Music that clowns danced around to.

'I don't even want to know what's going on in there,' said Angelo

'I do!' said Alan. 'It sounds like fun!'

Seth knocked on the garage door.

'I'M BUSY!' shouted Ryo from inside.

Seth looked around at the others.

'Knock again,' said Angelo.

'I thought you didn't want to see what was in there,' said Seth.

'I don't,' said Angelo. He grinned.

Seth knocked again.

'MUUUUUUM!' shouted Ryo. 'I TOLD YOU...'

The garage door lifted open.

Ryo was standing there dressed like a clown. An ACTUAL clown. Like the ones you see at kids' parties or fun fairs or in your nightmares. His face was painted white. His nose and lips were painted red. He had a green wig on, a multicoloured waistcoat, baggy pants and bowling shoes. 'You're not Mum,' he said. 'You go to my school. You're Seth.' He pointed at Seth, like Seth didn't know his own name.

'Are you a clown?' asked Alan. 'A real clown?'

Ryo shrugged. 'I wish.'

'Erm, sorry to bother you,' said Seth. 'But we wondered whether you wanted to play for our football team.'

'A football team?' asked Ryo. 'Just you guys?'

'No, there are some others,' said Seth. It felt good to say that. Even though it hadn't been straightforward or confirmed, things were sort of coming together. 'Sam Wall said he'll play. John...'

'The world's tallest boy,' Alan put in.

'From school?' asked Ryo.

Seth nodded. 'Curtis too.'

'I know Curtis,' said Ryo. 'He came here for tea once.'

'Just the once?' asked Seth.

'I think he found all the... this a bit weird,' said Ryo.

'I think it's awesome,' said Alan. 'Can you do any tricks?'

Ryo grinned. 'There is one trick I'm really good at.'

Seth didn't like the look of Ryo's grin.

'I'll show you,' said Ryo. He went into the garage.

Alan was inside before Seth could look around at the others and figure out what they were thinking.

Seth went inside too.

Beefy and Angelo followed.

Ryo closed the garage door behind them.

Inside, the garage was like being behind the scenes at a Big Top. There was a little table with a mirror and clown make-up, a rail full of brightly coloured clothes and a shelf filled with a bunch of creepy-looking ventriloquist dummies. It was possible that Ryo was now beating Alan in the weirdo stakes.

Alan raced over to the dummies. 'So cool!' he said. He picked up one of the dummies and put his hand up its back. 'I'm a dummy,' he said, in this strange robotic voice.

'No kidding,' said Seth.

The others laughed.

'So why are you, you know, a clown?' asked Beefy.

'I went to a fancy-dress party as a clown when I was little,' said Ryo. 'And I dunno, from then on I just wanted to be a clown. Dressing up like this makes me feel good.'

'Freaks me out,' said Seth. 'So what's this trick then?'

'I'll need a volunteer,' said Ryo.

Seth looked around at the others.

Beefy was looking down at the floor.

Angelo was looking up at the ceiling.

'I'll do it!' said Alan.

Seth felt relieved. For a moment he thought that he was going to have to volunteer for whatever creepy surprise it was Ryo had in store for them.

'What do I have to do?' asked Alan.

'Just stand over there,' said Ryo. He pointed at a large wooden board. It was painted white with a large red circle. Inside that circle, another red circle. And so on, until it was just a red spot.

Alan went over to the board.

'Stand with your back to it,' said Ryo. 'Hold those handles.'

Alan did as he was asked. He took hold of two black handles that jutted out at either end of the board.

'It looks like a target,' said Angelo.

'It is,' said Ryo.

'Target... for what?' asked Alan. He didn't sound as happy. He sounded pretty scared.

'Just these,' said Ryo. He went over to another shelf and took a handful of big, scary-looking knives.

Ryo was *definitely* beating Alan in the weirdo stakes. An eleven out of ten on the weird-o-meter.

'You're... you're going to throw those at me?' asked Alan.

'Clowns don't throw knives,' said Seth. 'Do they?'

'I do,' said Ryo.

'But you can't,' Seth cried. 'You'll kill him!'

'I won't,' said Ryo. He went over to Beefy and Angelo and gave them each a knife. 'What do you think?'

Angelo grinned. 'They're nice,' he said.

Beefy grinned too. 'Yeah. Really nice.'

'You think I can do it?' asked Ryo.

'Yeah, man,' said Angelo. 'I reckon you can.'

'No way,' said Seth. 'You're not throwing knives at him. He might be a weirdo, but he's our weirdo!' He stomped over to the target board and pulled Alan away.

'I'm good at this,' said Ryo. 'I won't hit him.'

'Good for you,' said Seth.

'If you don't let me show you, I won't join your team,' Ryo said.

'I don't care. We'll find someone else.'

'Like who?' asked Beefy.

'Someone,' said Seth. 'Anyone.'

'Just one knife,' said Ryo. 'Don't you trust me?'

'Not really,' said Seth. 'You're dressed like a clown.'

'Why don't you do it instead, Seth?' said Angelo. 'Let him throw one at you.'

'No way!'

'Go on,' said Beefy. 'For the Freaks.'

Seth eyeballed his two best mates. 'You for real?'

'For the Freaks,' Angelo repeated.

Seth rubbed his face in his hands and groaned. 'No way,' he said.

'But we need him,' said Beefy.

'Yeah, Sethy,' said Angelo.

Seth took a breath and thought about it. Ryo wouldn't throw knives at people if he wasn't any good at it. Surely? If this was what he had to do to wipe that grin off Daniel Logan's stupid face, maybe this was what he had to do. He swallowed. 'One knife,' he said to Ryo. 'And if it hits me, I swear, I'll take it and I'll shove it where the sun don't shine!'

'I won't hit you,' Ryo said calmly.

'You better not,' said Seth. He walked over to the target, put his back to the board and took hold of the handles.

DRINKING BLOOD

Ryo went over to his docking station. He took his iPod and changed tracks.

A drum roll started.

Seth felt his heart pounding almost as quickly as the drums. 'Really?' asked Seth. 'That's what you're gonna play?'

'Aim for his balls!' said Angelo.

Seth growled at him.

'On the count of three,' said Ryo. 'One. Two. Three.'

He threw the knife.

Seth squeezed his eyes shut.

He clenched his teeth.

He tensed every muscle in his body.

The knife hit him in his stomach.

Seth screamed out.

He expected pain.

Blood.

Death.

But there was no pain.

He opened his eyes.

The knife was on the floor.

There was no blood.

Or death for that matter.

Angelo was creased over. Beefy was howling. Alan was frowning.

Seth bent down and picked the knife up. It was light. Soft. Bendy. 'Is it rubber?' he asked.

Ryo gave him a big grin.

'Did you two know?' Seth asked Beefy and Angelo.

'You should've seen your face!' said Beefy, through tears of laughter.

'Idiots!' said Seth. He hurled the knife at the pair of them.

It just missed Angelo's head.

Alan came over to Seth and offered his hand. 'I thought you were very brave,' said Alan. 'You're my hero.'

Angelo and Beefy creased even more.

There was one last stop for the day. Goth Green.

Once they were off the bus, Seth walked through the town quickly. He was still really annoyed at his mates.

'Come on,' said Angelo. 'You'd have done the same.'

'Wouldn't,' Seth retorted.

'You would've,' said Beefy. 'And you know it.'

Maybe they were right. How could you turn down a wind up like that? They *were* right. He totally would've. 'Maybe,' he said.

'See,' said Angelo. 'You so would've.'

Seth started laughing and everyone joined in.

'You're still idiots,' said Seth.

It was just after four. Goth Green was a patch of grass in the centre of town. It was where the goths congregated on a Saturday. Hence the reason they called it Goth Green. Seth didn't know where this tradition started, but he always found it a bit weird that goths congregated on a patch of grass in town. He thought they should be in some basement of a derelict warehouse or a decrepit graveyard. But there they all were. About fifty of them. With their long black coats, their eye-liner and their dyed black hair that looked as though it needed a wash. All there. On a sunny Saturday afternoon. On a patch of grass in the middle of town.

Seth spotted Alex. He was pretty tall, but nowhere near Tall-John tall. He was wide too, but not as wide as Sam. He had long dark hair, pale skin and dark makeup around his eyes. He was wearing an old military-style jacket and big steel toe-capped boots.

'Are we sure this is a good idea?' asked Beefy. 'I mean after everything that's happened. What's he gonna want us to do? Drink blood? Sacrifice baby pigs to the devil?'

'This is like a video game,' said Angelo. 'We have to do something to get them to do something. You know what I mean?'

'It's like a quest,' said Alan. 'Like *Lord of the Rings*. Isn't it? Except we don't have a ring. Do we?'

Seth shook his head.

'And we aren't Hobbits,' said Alan.

'You do look a bit like a Hobbit,' Seth told him.

'Do I?'

'A bit.'

Alan grinned.

Seth led the way through the gathering of goths.

Alex was talking to two older-looking goth girls. They were both quite fit and they looked a fair bit older than Alex. Maybe even sixteen or seventeen. One had bright red hair and black lipstick. The other had black, curly hair and she was wearing a short, tartan skirt.

Seth stopped in front of them. He felt pretty awkward. This was the hardest one yet.

They stopped talking and each turned to Seth.

'Hi, Alex,' said Seth.

'Hi,' said Alex.

'We go to the same school.'

'Yeah,' said Alex. 'I've seen you.'

'I was wondering,' Seth began. '*We* were wondering...' He gestured over his shoulder at his mates. 'Whether you wanted to play for our football team?'

'Football?'

'You don't know anything about it, right?'

'Not really,' Alex said.

'But you'll join us if we do something for you?' said Seth.

'I don't want to drink any blood,' said Alan. 'I don't like blood.'

Alex frowned and smiled.

The girls smiled too.

'Why would I want you to do something for me?' asked Alex.

'Just the way things are done, isn't it?' Seth shrugged.

'I'll play for you,' said Alex.

'You what?' asked Seth.

'I'll play,' Alex repeated.

'You will?' asked Seth. 'Really?'

'Yeah,' said Alex.

'Just like that?' said Seth.

Alex shrugged.

Seth stared at Alex. Then the girls. 'Is this

a joke?'

'No joke,' said Alex. 'Just give me the details. It'll be fun. Won't it?'

Seth blinked. 'Yeah. Fun. Definitely.'

'Awesome,' said Alex. He held his hand out.

Seth blinked again. Then he shook Alex's hand.

The others shook Alex's hand too.

Seth gave Alex the details and the boys left.

'Well that was easy,' said Beefy, as they headed back to the bus stop.

Seth nodded.

'It was, wasn't it?'

'I guess some people are just nice, you know,' said Angelo. 'Just wanna get involved and that.'

Seth smirked and shook his head.

The next day, Seth and the others met up at the allotment not far from his house. There were lots of little plots growing all types of things. Flowers. Vegetables. Fruit. Some even had pigs and chickens.

'I didn't know they had all this business here,' said Angelo.

'What business?' asked Seth.

'Pigs and that,' said Angelo.

'Must be where Alex gets them,' said Seth. 'To sacrifice to the devil.'

Sam appeared up ahead. 'Hey. This way, guys,' he said.

Seth and the others followed him along to his grandad's plot.

'How do, fellas,' said Sam's grandad. He was wearing wellies and dungarees. 'Hope you've bought a strong stomach with you.'

'Strong stomach?' asked Seth. 'What for?'

'For shifting that lot,' said Sam's grandad. He pointed at a huge pile of manure.

Seth swallowed. 'Is that...'

'Manure,' said Sam's grandad. 'The finest around these parts.'

'Is this a wind up?' asked Beefy.

Sam grinned. He shook his head.

Seth swallowed. He rolled up his sleeves. 'Come on,' he said. 'Let's get shovelling.'

The closer they got to the pile of manure, the stronger the smell.

'Man,' said Angelo. 'It stinks worse than Beef's farts!'

Angelo was spot on. The pile of poo was an easy nine on the stink-o-meter.

'The things we're doing for this football team, eh?' said Beefy.

Seth patted his friend on the back. 'I know,' he said. 'But it'll all be worth it.'

'I hope you're right.'

'Me too.'

'If you eat horse poo,' said Alan, 'does it make you grow?'

'Dunno,' said Seth. 'Why don't you try?'

Alan looked at the pile of manure, as he considered. 'I'm not that hungry,' he said.

Once they were done shovelling the manure, Sam's grandad thanked the boys for their help and Sam agreed to turn up for the next training session.

The boys left the allotment and headed home.

'I so need a shower,' said Angelo.

Beefy nodded. 'Me too.'

'That makes three of us,' Seth added.

Seth waited for Alan to add his little joke in, but Alan just grinned.

'Just one more player then,' said Angelo.

'Yep,' said Beefy. 'One more.'

'Just the one,' said Seth.

Alan grinned. 'Do you mean Jordan?' he asked.

No one said anything.

THE BIG ONE

The following Monday, the boys met up outside
the school gates once school had finished. Seth
realised they were meeting at the school gates a
lot. It was hard work making a football team. He
didn't realise all the things he'd have to get into.
Being a spy. Doing homework. Having knives
thrown at him. Shovelling horse crap. When
he'd suggested they make their own team, he
hadn't counted on just how much hard work it
would be. He wondered whether it would all be
worth the effort. He hoped it would, for all their
sakes.

And now there was this: The Big One. Jordan
McGrath.

Alan unzipped his bags. He pulled out the
fake moustache and glasses and offered it to
Seth.

Seth waved it away. 'No disguises today,' he
said. There was no way he was approaching

Jordan while wearing a fake moustache. Jordan would definitely think he was on a wind up. Jordan wasn't someone you wanted to wind up.

'Yeah, I'm with Seth,' said Beefy. 'I'm not going up to Jordan dressed as a werewolf.'

Alan sighed. 'Well, at least take these,' he said. He handed Seth a few business cards. 'For Jordan.'

Seth took the cards and put them in his pocket.

'Anyone seen him?' asked Angelo.

'I saw him earlier,' said Seth. 'In science class. He got a detention for giving Mr Thatcher some cheek.'

'Nice,' said Angelo. He grinned.

'So are we gonna just hang around?' asked Beefy.

Seth shrugged. 'Guess so.'

The lads found a spot around the corner of the building, where they could keep an eye on the entrance. Everyone was really quiet. Even Alan wasn't his usual chatty self. Seth knew the reason why. They were all nervous. None of them wanted to go up to Jordan McGrath and ask him to play for their team. Seth knew though, out of all the players on his list, Jordan was the best. With him in the side, they'd have a chance against Logan's lot. It would be a small chance, admittedly, but more of a chance than they'd have without him.

'You know,' said Seth, 'we don't have to do this.'

'We don't?' asked Beefy.

'But then we won't have a full team,' Angelo said.

'I know,' said Seth. 'But we've worked really hard and I think that if we really don't want to do this, we should give ourselves a break.'

'No,' said Alan. 'We need one more player. Don't we?'

Seth looked around. He nodded.

Alan was eyeballing him. 'And we want this player. Don't we?'

Seth nodded again.

'Well we should get him!' said Alan.

'Big Al's right,' said Angelo. 'We've come this far. We can do this, can't we?'

Seth nodded.

'Go on, then,' said Beefy.

'Let's do that thing,' said Alan. 'This is where we all put our hands in!' He put his hand in.

'Still no,' said Seth.

Alan made a pathetic puppy-dog noise.

Just at that moment, Jordan appeared from the main entrance.

'Shush, lads, look,' said Seth.

They watched him as he walked through the gates.

'We definitely sure about this?' asked Beefy.

'Come on,' said Seth.

The lads followed Jordan to the old industrial estate on the outskirts of town. The place was filled with abandoned warehouse buildings, rusted fences and rubble. The sky had become overcast with grey clouds. It was starting to get cold.

Seth had goosebumps on his arms.

'You don't think he knows we're following him, does he?' whispered Beefy. 'He might be leading us into a trap.'

'You don't think it's a trap, do you?' asked Angelo.

'Course not,' said Seth, even though he wasn't sure he believed himself.

'Do you think he's going to kill us?' whispered Beefy. 'He looks like he could definitely kill us.'

'I think you need to stop watching late-night TV,' said Seth. 'It's broken your brain.'

'I'm just saying,' said Beefy. 'This is definitely somewhere a murderer would bring his victims.'

Up ahead, Jordan hauled his bag off his shoulder. He unzipped it and pulled out a battered old football. He dumped his bag on the ground and blasted the ball against the wall of an old factory.

In that moment, Seth's opinion of Jordan shifted a bit. He looked pretty lonely, kicking the ball against the wall on his own. It was sort of sad. Seth remembered a few occasions when he'd done the same against the wall of the old house where he used to live. He wondered whether he'd looked that sad and lonely to anybody walking by.

'What's he doing?' asked Beefy.

'What's it look like?' said Seth. 'He's playing squash.'

Seth watched as Jordan kicked the ball against the wall. He took the ball on his chest and volleyed it with real power.

'He does have skills,' said Beefy.

'Mad skills,' said Angelo.

'Go and ask him if he wants to be a Freak then, Seth,' said Beefy.

'You go,' said Seth. 'Why's it always me that has to do everything?'

'Go on,' said Angelo. 'Man up!'

'You man up!' said Seth. 'I'm not doing it.' He folded his arms. Now he was here, he didn't want to go over to someone who looked like they'd had their head dragged through a car park and ask them whether they wanted to be a Freak.

'Please, Seth,' said Alan. 'You're our leader.' He had his hands clasped together in front of him as though he was praying.

Angelo and Beefy had desperate looks on their faces too.

'For the Freaks,' said Beefy.

'Yeah, man. The Freaks,' said Angelo.

'Stop saying that, will you,' said Seth.

Beefy gave him a sad smile.

Angelo widened his eyes and fluttered his eyelashes like some cartoon character.

Seth sighed. He looked at his mates' stupid faces. What else could he do?

'OK,' said Seth. 'I'll go and talk to the school psycho!' He took a breath, composed himself and marched over to Jordan McGrath. As he got closer, he found that he was doing less of a march and more of a tiptoe. He looked back at the others.

They were all nodding and waving him forward.

He turned back towards Jordan as he blasted the ball hard against the wall.

Seth swallowed. For some reason, his head was filled with images of Jordan blasting the football against his face.

As he got to about twenty metres away, he coughed.

Jordan paid no attention. He juggled the ball, then volleyed it hard against the wall again.

Seth coughed again. This time louder.

Jordan trapped the ball under his foot and turned around.

'Erm, hi,' said Seth. 'I... you're... we go to the same school... I was wondering whether you... whether you wanted to play for a football team, with me and my friends back there?' Seth flicked his thumb over his shoulder.

Seth's mates grinned and waved. They looked like a bunch of fools.

Jordan snorted and spat on the floor.

'Well,' said Seth. 'I don't want to disturb you, from your... thing. But if you're interested, we train on Wednesday nights from six thirty, over on Barrowby Field.'

'GIVE HIM A CARD!' shouted Alan.

'Erm...' Seth reached into his pocket. He pulled out one of the cards Alan had given him. He stepped towards Jordan as though he was approaching a growling dog. He offered Jordan the card. He did his best to stop his hand from trembling. There, boy, that's a good Jordan, he thought.

Jordan took the card from him. 'How much?' he asked.

'How much what?' asked Seth.

'Money,' said Jordan. 'How much will you pay me?'

'Erm, we hadn't planned on paying you,' said Seth.

Jordan turned away from Seth and kicked the ball against the wall again.

Seth backed away. Then he turned to leave. He stopped. He turned back to Jordan. 'We've got a big game against Daniel Logan and the school team. If you play for us, I'll give you... a tenner?'

'Twenty,' said Jordan

'Fifteen?' asked Seth.

'Twenty.'

'OK,' said Seth. 'Twenty quid, if you play. Only if you play though.'

Jordan blasted the ball against the wall again.

Seth turned away. He didn't turn back this time though. He almost ran back to his friends.

'Well,' said Angelo. 'What did he say?'

'He'll play in the match.'

'For real?'

'For twenty quid.'

'Oh,' said Beefy.

Seth shrugged. 'Fiver each.'

'Fair enough,' said Angelo.

'We've got a team now, haven't we?' asked Alan. 'A full team?'

Seth thought about it. 'Yeah, we do.'

'That's pretty sweet, Sethy,' said Angelo. He held his fist out.

Seth bumped it.

'Shall we put our hands in now?' asked Alan.

Seth glanced back at Jordan. 'We're never going to do that,' said Seth. He put his arm around Alan and led him away.

FREAKS UN-UNITED

The following Wednesday, they headed over to the field.

Steve carried the holdall as the boys walked beside him.

Seth was pleased that they'd been able to assemble eleven players, but he knew there was a big difference between having eleven players and having a team. It might turn out to be nothing more than a ridiculous freak show and a big waste of time. And they would look even more like idiots.

'You should see it, Stevie,' said Angelo. 'Seth thought it was an actual knife. It was hilarious.'

'It wasn't that funny,' said Seth.

'No,' said Angelo. 'It was.'

'It was,' said Beefy.

'Whatever, man,' said Seth.

'But we've got eleven players?' asked Steve. 'You're sure about that?'

'As long as they all turn up,' Seth replied.

'They're proper freaks too!' said Angelo. 'There's a really tall one and a really fast one and this one that looks like something from a Halloween party!'

'And there's this scary psycho one as well,' said Beefy.

'And there's one who dresses like a clown,' said Angelo.

'Sounds like you picked a strong bunch,' said a smirking Steve.

When they got onto the field Alan, Laura, Curtis, Alex and Ryo were already there.

Angelo whispered to Seth. 'She's so hot.'

'She's OK,' whispered Seth.

'OK?' said Angelo. 'Are you mental? She's bootilicious!'

Seth let out a laugh. He felt positive. From a distance, everyone who was there looked dressed for football. But as he got closer, he realised Games Workshop boy Curtis was wearing loafers. And Alex was wearing his big steel toe-capped goth boots. At least Ryo hadn't come in his clown make-up. That was something. This is gonna be hard work, he thought.

When the group came together, Alan patted Seth on the back. 'We'll beat Daniel and his lot,' he said. 'With these guys, they've got no chance!'

'I dunno,' Seth replied. 'Guys, I don't mean to be harsh or anything. But your shoes. You're not gonna be able to play in those.'

'What do you mean?' asked Curtis. 'What's wrong with these bad boys?' He lifted one of his feet and twisted his loafer around for everyone to see.

'They're lovely,' said Alan.

'But what I think Seth's trying to say is,' said Steve, 'they might not be the best for a kick-about.'

'Oh,' said Curtis. 'That's disappointing.'

'I still think they're lovely,' said Alan.

'Tell me your sizes before we finish,' said Steve. 'I'll sort you out some boots for next week.'

Laura sniggered.

Seth felt his heart sink a bit. Whatever happened with the Freaks, it felt like it was his responsibility. It was his idea after all. He was taking the lead on most stuff. If it all went pear-shaped, it was him who was going to look an idiot.

Slowly, but surely, the other Freaks arrived.

First came Sam, wearing a Barcelona shirt and shorts. He was easily the most normal of the new recruits. His calves were huge. All that muck shovelling must have been good for the muscles.

'He's a big lad,' commented Steve.

Then came Homework John. He was wearing a T-shirt that said 'Atari' on it and shorts. They weren't quite as short as Steele's, but they were on the way. Seth figured shorts would always look shorter on someone with such ridiculously long legs.

'He's a big lad too!' Steve said.

Seth was a little anxious about what footwear John had brought, so he was relieved when John pulled out a pair of size fifteen Nikes. They might've been the size of clown shoes, but at least they were actual trainers.

'Look at those!' gasped Angelo, when he saw the trainers. 'You could live in them!'

Alan creased at this. He laughed so hard, Seth thought he might have a nosebleed.

'What does your mum feed you?' Steve asked John.

'I bet he's been eating the manure off Sam's allotment!' said Beefy.

'Does it make you grow that much?' asked Alan.

'I think the story goes that you grow if you put manure in your shoes,' said Steve.

'John's mum could get enough manure in those beasts!' said Angelo, pointing at John's trainers.

Everyone laughed. Except John.

Seth patted John on the back. 'You'll get used to it,' he said.

Even though the Freaks were an odd-looking bunch with their loafers and steel toe-capped boots, there were enough of them to make a team. Almost. Everyone except Jordan had arrived.

'There's only ten of us,' said Laura. 'Who's missing?'

'Jordan McGrath,' said Seth.

Curtis and Ryo whispered to one another.

'Is he that boy in your year?' asked Laura. 'The hot one?'

'He's not hot,' said Seth.

'He is.'

'Yeah, he is!' said Alan.

Seth frowned.

'At football, I mean,' Alan went on. 'He's hot at football.'

'Do you think he'll come?' asked Laura.

Seth shrugged. Now he was here, with everyone assembled, a part of him didn't want Jordan to come. Okay, he had skills, there was no doubting that. But Jordan might be cheeky to his dad or cause trouble and that wouldn't be cool. And now there was the added possibility that Laura had a thing for Jordan. Deep down, Seth knew he didn't really have any chance with Laura, but if things went well with the Freaks and he was top dog, she might start seeing him differently. She might think he had something about him. It was unlikely, but he knew with Jordan on the team, he would never be top dog.

'Right,' said Steve, once everyone had done their stretches. 'I want you in two teams. New players against the original lot. And Laura.'

'There's Jordan!' shouted Alan.

Seth looked up.

'JORDAN!' shouted Alan. 'OVER HERE!'

Jordan was indeed walking across the field towards them. He was wearing a plain black T-shirt, black tracksuit pants and a New York Yankees snapback.

'We'll have Jordan,' Laura said to Seth's dad.

'That's fine,' said Steve. 'I'll go in goal for the other side then.'

'Jordan Jordan Jordan,' Angelo whispered to Seth. 'Why doesn't she marry him?'

Jordan dumped his backpack behind the goalposts with the others and sat down.

'All right,' Steve said to him.

Jordan nodded.

'You playing?' asked Steve.

'I'll just watch,' Jordan replied.

'He's so enigmatic, isn't he?' said Laura.

'He's what?' asked Angelo.

'Mysterious,' said Laura.

Angelo looked at Seth and rolled his eyes up into his skull.

Seth smirked.

Steve clapped his hands together a few times. 'OK, everyone. Before you all leave tonight, I'll have to get your folks' details. I don't want any of them worrying about where you are or anything.'

John coughed. 'Is there any chance you could tell my parents... that I'm getting extra tuition. They're not... they don't think football's a good use of my time.'

'I dunno, mate,' Steve replied.

'Go on, Big Steve,' said Angelo.

'How about this?' said Steve. 'I'll pop a few general knowledge questions at you as we go?'

John beamed. 'That sounds great!'

'Could you ask me some too?' asked Ryo.

'And me?' asked Curtis.

Steve scratched his head. 'Sure,' he said.

Seth shook his head. He wondered if he should have started a science club instead.

Steve took his place in goal and booted the ball.

The original Freaks started off knocking the ball about.

Angelo picked up the ball. He did a step-over and glided past Ryo.

Seth called for it.

Angelo laid it off to Seth.

Seth beat Alex, and then squared the ball to Alan.

Alan lashed at the ball, but sent it way wide of the goal. He fell back on the grass.

Seth helped him up. He patted Alan on the back. 'You'll get it,' he said.

'Will I?' asked Alan.

'Yeah, man, course,' said Seth.

Steve caught Seth's eye. He nodded at Seth and gave him a wink before kicking the ball out again.

Alex got a hold of it and passed it to Ryo.

Ryo hit a long one to Curtis.

Curtis flailed at the ball, completely missing it. His loafer went flying off through the goal.

Laura burst out laughing. Some of the others did too.

Jordan sniggered. He grabbed his bag and stood up.

'You going?' asked Steve.

Jordan raised his eyebrows and walked away.

'Not going very well, is it?' Beefy said to Seth.

Seth had to agree. 'Not really.'

Once Jordan had left, things went from bad to worse. The passing was awful. The tackling was a joke. The shooting didn't bear thinking about. The Freaks were a shambles. A huge, horrible mess.

As Seth and his dad trudged across the field on their way home, Seth knew there was no way they'd be able to get a team out of the players he'd assembled.

'Good session,' said Steve.

'Was it?' asked Seth.

'It was a start.'

'You wouldn't believe the things we had to do to get that lot there tonight.'

'I know, mate,' said Steve. 'You've worked really hard.'

'For what though?' asked Seth. 'We're gonna get slaughtered when we play the school team.'

'There's a couple of weeks yet,' said Steve. 'Still time.'

'I doubt it.'

'Look, mate. These things take a while. You've got eleven players together in a week. On your own. That's an accomplishment in itself.'

'You reckon?'

'I do, yeah.'

'It's just,' said Seth, 'I really want to win, you know. I want to show Logan and Steele that we can play.'

'And you'll do that,' said Steve.

'Not if we play like we did tonight.'

'No, but I'd be surprised if you were that bad again.'

'I wouldn't.'

FREAKS UNITED

At school, the following day, Seth saw a few of the Freaks around the place. Tall John gave him a nod. Sam smiled. Ryo grinned. It was as though they were members of some secret club. The worst football club ever created. OK, that might've been pushing it. There were probably at least four worse football teams out there. Somewhere. Made up of under-sevens. There had to be.

Seth sat with Beefy, Angelo and Alan on the school field, eating their packed lunches. It'd been a few weeks since the knock back from the school team and he could just about face the field now.

Seth ate his cheese and onion sandwich. It was one of his favourites. Two slices of crusty bread. A thick slice of cheese and lots of onion. His dad made the best sandwiches.

Angelo was drinking a can of energy drink

called Bezerker. Seth was amazed that Angelo's mum let him have the stuff. Angelo didn't need any more energy.

Beefy was eating a sandwich too. But the bread was brown and there seemed to be salad sticking out of the sides.

'Are you still eating salad?' Seth asked him.

'Huh huh.'

'You're taking this diet thing seriously, aren't you?'

Beefy nodded. He took another bite from his sandwich and screwed his face up a bit. 'I wish it was cake.'

They laughed.

Seth watched as Logan and his mates played football across the field. Logan was doing his usual tricks and skills.

There were girls sitting behind the goals, talking and giggling. One of the girls was called Elle. She was in Seth's class. Seth was sure she was the fittest girl in his year. She was even fitter than Laura. A solid ten on the fit-o-meter. It might sound odd, but Elle clearly had a thing for pink. She had pink hair. Pink nails. Pink earrings. She had nice tanned skin and she wore cool-looking Converse. Pink too. Obviously. Some people might've thought her obsession with pink was odd. Seth thought it was cool. It made her stand out from every other girl in his year. Of course, she'd like Logan. They were a perfect match. Him and his hair. Her and her pink stuff. Seth didn't want to admit it, but he was jealous of Logan. The fact that Elle liked Logan only made Seth hate him more.

'Not long till we play them,' said Beefy. 'Do you think we've got any chance?'

'Course we have,' said Angelo. 'They'll underestimate us, just like we did when we played the girls. That's when we'll crush them!' He smacked his fist against the palm of his other hand and twisted it, gritting his teeth.

'You reckon?' asked Seth. 'Even after the last session?'

Angelo screwed his face up. 'Yeah. Why not?' He didn't sound as confident this time though.

'So where do you think everyone will play?' Beefy asked.

'That's up to my dad,' said Seth.

'Stevie will play me in midfield,' said Angelo. 'He thinks I've got a good engine.'

'Where do you think he'll play you, mate?' asked Beefy.

'I don't care,' said Seth. 'I'll play anywhere he wants me to.'

The bell rang out so they packed their bits up and picked themselves up off the ground.

Seth knocked the bits of grass off his backside. He took another look over at Elle and Logan. The pair of them were talking and laughing. Gutted, Seth and his mates made their way across the field, towards school.

As they walked along the corridor that led to their form room, someone shouted.

'Yo, Freaks!'

Seth turned around.

Logan and his henchmen, Foreman and Mendes, were walking behind them. Logan bounced a football on the floor. 'Saw you spying on us again at dinner time,' he said.

'We weren't spying.'

'Whatever,' said Logan. 'Like it makes any difference. Bet you haven't even got enough players to make a team.'

'We have, actually,' said Angelo.

Foreman grunted like a caveman. Mendes narrowed his eyelids over his bug eyes.

'Look at them,' Logan smirked. 'Getting all cocky. Do you really think you've got a chance?'

'Yeah,' said Angelo. 'We've got a chance.'

'You lot really are freaks,' said Logan. 'We're gonna destroy you. We're gonna make you look stupid.'

'What?' asked Angelo. 'Just like you?'

'You what?' Logan stepped closer. His words

were a growl now.

Foreman and Mendes stepped forward too.

Seth looked from Logan's square jaw, which he'd pushed forward, to Foreman's big clenched fists, to Mendes' narrowed bug eyes.

'Just leave it,' Seth said to Angelo.

'Yeah, just leave it,' said Logan. 'Listen to your friend.'

'Why should we?' Angelo whispered to Seth. 'I'm sick of him.'

'I know, but...'

'Everything all right, boys?' asked a voice.

Jordan was standing alongside Seth and his mates now.

Logan looked at Jordan for a moment. He swallowed. 'Come on, lads,' he said. He led his crew past Seth and away down the corridor. 'We'll see you out on the pitch,' he called, once he was safe distance away.

'We will,' said Seth.

Logan flicked his head and they all carried on.

Jordan walked off down the corridor in the opposite direction.

'Being a Freak might have some uses after all!' said Beefy.

Seth was busy. Crazy busy. If he wasn't training,

he was doing homework club with John or gaming with Curtis or helping Sam down at the allotment. He was enjoying getting to know all the new players. Sam was a down-to-earth lad who liked most of the same things as Seth and his mates. John was serious about school work, but when he wasn't being serious, he was a good laugh. Curtis was funny too. And for the first time since Seth had started at Tommy Moon, he felt like he had a bunch of mates. They might not have been the best football team — they mightn't have even resembled a football team — but they were a good bunch of lads. And Laura, of course. The luscious Laura. He got to hang out with her too. She made him forget about Logan and Elle and their giggling.

At the next training session, the Freaks gathered on the field again for training. Seth was pleased. He'd expected some of them to not turn up after their shocking first session. If he hadn't been responsible for the team, he probably wouldn't have bothered turning up himself. The only player who hadn't arrived was Jordan. Seth hadn't expected anything else. They were probably going to have to find another player and time was ticking away. Still, Seth hoped that the promise of twenty quid would be enough of an incentive for Jordan to at least turn up to The Big Match against Logan's lot.

'So?' said Steve. 'How's everyone feeling?'

'OK,' said Seth.

'Confident?'

'Not really,' said Beefy.

'Come on, Beef,' said Steve. 'You've gotta have some belief in yourself.'

'I would if we weren't so crap.'

There were a few sniggers.

'It's gonna take a bit of time, that's all.' Steve told them. 'A good team is better than the sum of its parts.'

'Big Stevie, you're talking in riddles,' said Angelo.

'All I mean is,' Steve went on, 'individually, OK, there's work that needs to be done. But as a team, if you stick together – play for one another – you could be good. Won't be easy. But nothing is.'

Seth felt himself cheer up a bit. He didn't have great confidence in his team-mates, but he did have confidence in his dad. Maybe Steve was right. Maybe they could be a team.

'There's Jordan!' cried Alan. He pointed over at the play area.

Seth didn't believe it until he saw Jordan himself, crossing the field. He had the same gear on as the last session.

Laura smiled.

Seth felt a mixture of optimism and disappointment. He was optimistic that if they did get Jordan playing, they might have a chance. And he was disappointed that it was Jordan he was pinning all his hopes on.

Jordan dumped his bag in the pile behind the goals.

'You playing this week, kidda?' Steve asked.

Jordan shrugged and made his way onto the pitch.

'Good,' said Steve. He went into his large holdall and pulled out a couple of pairs of football boots. 'Alex, Curtis, over here.'

The two lads went over and put on their boots.

Seth nodded at Jordan.

Jordan didn't nod back.

Laura smiled at Jordan.

Jordan gave her a half-smile in return.

Seth growled a little in the back of his throat.

'You OK?' asked Angelo.

Seth nodded.

'Right. Two teams,' Steve said, once he'd got them all to do a bit of stretching. 'Jordan. You and... Laura, you pick teams.'

Laura frowned.

Seth grinned at Angelo and Beefy.

'I'll have him,' said Jordan. He pointed at Angelo.

'Nice one,' said Angelo.

'Seth,' said Laura.

Seth winked at Angelo as he made his way over to Laura.

'You,' said Jordan. He pointed at Sam.

'Pick Beefy,' Seth whispered to Laura.

'Beefy,' she said.

Beefy joined the team. He bumped fists with Seth.

Jordan picked Ryo, Curtis and John.

Laura picked Alex and Alan. OK, she didn't really pick Alan. But Seth kind of liked having Alan on the team anyway.

'I'll go in goal for Laura's team,' said Steve. 'Even it up a bit.'

The game kicked off.

Angelo knocked the ball to Sam.

Sam played it out to Jordan.

Jordan cut inside. He beat Beefy, then Alex. Then he back-heeled the ball to Curtis.

Curtis whacked it.

His shoes didn't come flying off this time.

Instead the ball smacked against the crossbar.

Laura took the ball and cleared it.

'Effort!' called Steve.

Seth smiled. It was an effort. 'Where'd that

137

come from?' he asked Curtis.

Curtis shrugged. 'Dunno,' he said.

Seth held his fist out.

Curtis bumped it.

They played for an hour. In the end Jordan's side won fifteen-ten, but it was a good game. It was totally different to the first session. It was a lot more positive. All of the Freaks brought something different to the team. Laura had skills and she was a leader. Jordan had skills too, but he was more of a team player, which Seth found odd, because he didn't seem like much of a team player off the pitch. In fact, Jordan seemed OK. For a psycho. Big Sam was strong. Curtis was lightning fast. John was an OK target man. Even Alan was getting better. A bit. OK, he wasn't really. But he was trying and he was having fun and his enthusiasm was infectious.

Seth, Beefy and Angelo walked home with Steve.

'Now that *was* a good session,' Steve declared.

'Better than the last one,' said Angelo.

'Deffo,' added Beefy.

Seth laughed. 'Couldn't have been any worse!'

'I told you you'd get better, son,' said Steve. 'You did really well, boys. Getting a team together so quick. I'm proud of you.'

Seth beamed. He was dead proud too. He'd had doubts about the whole setting-up-their-own-team thing, but the session had gone well. Better than could ever be expected. Things were looking up. For now, at least.

THE BIG MATCH

The Big Game was looming. Seth tried not to think about the match, but it was on his mind all day long. All day at school. All evening. He kept repeating the scene in his head. Final minute. He'd rounded the keeper and stroked the ball into an open net. The Freaks had won. Everyone went wild. Laura and Elle both gave him big kisses. Sounded good, right?

The problem was, he'd allowed himself to believe. At least when he thought the Freaks would get annihilated, he could prepare for it. But training was going well and the fact that they had a few decent players was giving him hope. Usually, Seth would be happy to have some hope, but now, if they did lose, it would hurt so much more.

It was the evening of the Big Match. Steve had called a pre-match meeting at the house. The whole team were sitting in the living room. On the arms of chairs. On the floor. Wherever there was a space. Even Jordan had turned up. He was stood behind the sofa, quiet and moody as ever.

Seth sat on his usual spot on the sofa. It was his house after all.

Steve stood in front of them, with his arms folded. 'Now, boys, and Laura...'

Laura grinned.

'...I wanted to have a few words with you. I know we've only been together for a couple of weeks, but I just wanted to tell you how pleased and proud I am of you all.'

Seth grinned at Angelo and Beefy.

They both grinned back.

'When Seth said he wanted to start his own team,' Steve continued, 'I thought he was talking out of his backside. But, fair play to the lad. He's got you all together. And fair play to the rest of you. You're a great bunch and you're a team now too. And it doesn't matter what happens this evening. Win, lose, draw, I want you to go out there and have fun. Enjoy it. You deserve it.'

'Hear, hear, Big Stevie!' said Angelo.

Everyone laughed.

'Now, there's another thing,' said Steve. 'A team should really have a strip. So, I spoke with my boss.' He walked out of the room and went into the kitchen. A moment later, he returned with a box and pulled out a shirt. It was red, with black stripes, like an AC Milan shirt. Steve tossed the shirt to Seth.

Seth held it up, as all the other kids gathered around. The material felt good, just like his United shirt. It had a sponsor on the front too – Johnson's Builders. The best thing, though, was that there was a team badge on the chest. It was a little freaky face, with one big eye and a tongue hanging out. The word 'Freaks' was written above the head in yellow letters. It said 'United' below. It was one of the most awesome things Seth had ever seen.

'That is soooooo cool,' said Beefy.

Seth finally looked up. 'Who did the badge?'

'You can thank resident artist, Big Al, for that,' Steve replied.

Alan got lots of pats on the back, a few 'nice ones' and a couple of awkward high-fives. Alan still hadn't mastered the art of the high-five.

'I know it should've been a team decision,' said Steve. 'But I wanted it to be a surprise for you all.'

Seth was grinning from ear to ear. 'No, this is totally cool,' he said.

'Really cool,' said Angelo.

'You've all got one,' Steve told them. He began handing them around to each of the players. Each shirt had a nickname on the back. Beefy's said, well, 'Beefy'. Angelo's said 'Raging Bull'. Seth's said 'Captain Hart'.

Captain Hart, thought Seth. It made him sound like a superhero. That worked.

'So, you want the job?' asked Steve.

'Duh,' said Seth. 'Of course!'

Seth got a few pats on the back himself this time.

There was lots of back-patting going on. Seth thought back to all the back-patting exchanged between the lads who'd been selected for the school team. He hadn't liked that. This back-patting was OK though. The Freaks deserved a bit of back-patting.

All of the Freaks loved their shirts. Sam's said 'Big Sam' on the back. Alex's said 'Be Scared'. Ryo's said 'Silks' and Curtis' said 'Speedy'. Laura's said 'The Guv'nor'. Jordan's said 'Tekkers'. John's said 'Long John'. They all pulled their shirts on, over their own tops.

'Take a picture, Stevie!' said Angelo.

The team gathered around the sofa.

Steve pulled his phone out and took aim. 'Say "Freaks",' he said.

Everyone shouted 'FREAKS!' apart from

Jordan.

The phone made a click.

'We can put that on my website!' said Alan. 'My fans will love it!' His shirt had 'Big Al' on the back.

The team walked over to the playing field. It was a quarter past six. Fifteen minutes until kick-off. They followed Steve through their stretches.

Once they were all limbered up and loose, they kicked the ball about. Their passing was sharp and accurate.

Seth looked around at his team-mates. OK, they still looked like an odd bunch – all shapes and sizes and colours – but now they were wearing their shirts, they looked like a proper team. The hope that they might win began to swell inside him. He couldn't stop it. It was eleven against eleven and all those things the pundits said when little teams played big teams flashed through his head. And if they played to their best, they had a chance. A *real* chance.

Even though it'd only been a few weeks, they'd all made progress.

Beefy seemed to have lost a bit of weight.

Angelo was definitely calmer.

Seth felt faster and fitter.

Even Alan could sort of control a ball now.

Sort of.

'Right,' said Steve. 'Gather round. I want to give you the team.'

He pulled a piece of paper from his pocket. 'You're all playing as there's only eleven of you. So, please don't get injured. Take it easy, OK? That means you, Ange.'

'I'll take it easy,' said Angelo. 'Don't you worry.'

Steve grinned.

'OK. So Sam, you'll be in goal...'

Sam nodded.

'Beefy and Alex, I want you to play central defence.'

Beefy looked over at Alex and nodded.

Alex nodded back.

Lots of nods, thought Seth. Everyone looked serious. The Freaks meant business.

'Ryo, you're right back, and Alan, you're left.'

'I won't let you down, Steve,' said Alan.

'I know you won't,' Steve replied. 'Laura, Angelo, I want you two central midfield. Don't give them any time on the ball. I want you, Curtis, on the left, and on the right, Jordan. I want you both to go at their full-backs every time you get the ball.'

Curtis nodded.

Jordan sniffed.

'Up top, John and Seth,' Steve finished.

Seth grinned. He was dead pleased he'd at least get the chance to slam the ball in the back of the net. And slam Logan's words down his throat.

Seth and John slapped hands.

'Stay close,' said John. 'I'll get the knock-ons. That's right isn't it? "Knock-ons"?'

'That's right,' said Seth, still grinning.

'Who are we?' asked Steve.

'Freaks?' replied Angelo.

'I can't hear you!' Steve shouted.

They all shouted back together. 'FREAKS!'

Seth was psyched. He felt well up for it. They all looked like they were. Even Alan was making growling noises. Actually, they were more like 'garr-ing' noises. He'd clearly mixed up pit-bulls with pirates.

Then Seth saw a crowd heading across the field. Not only had Logan got the school team in their blue and white strips, but there was a bunch of other kids from school, including some of the girls from Seth's form. Elle was there. She was wearing a little pink top, a short denim skirt and her Cons.

Worst of all, they were being led by Steele.

Seth didn't feel so up for it any more.

ANNIHILATION

The crowd arrived near the Freaks at the side of the pitch.

Logan sneered at Seth.

'Who's that?' asked Steve, flicking his head in Steele's direction.

'That's Mr Steele,' said Seth reluctantly.

Steve inhaled slowly.

'That's him, is it?'

'Don't do anything stupid.'

'I won't,' Steve replied. 'Don't worry.'

Steele came over, with his team following behind. He was wearing his super-short shorts again. Seth tried not to look, but he couldn't stop himself. They were almost like hot pants.

'Who are you?' Steele asked Steve.

'I'm this lad's dad,' Steve replied. He patted Seth on the shoulder. 'You know, the lad you called a freak.'

'Now, hold on a minute,' said Steele. 'I...'

'Look,' Steve cut him off. 'If I'd have had my way, I'd have been down that school and we'd have been having words. Now, my boy, he didn't want that. He's a lot nicer than I am, see?'

'Are you threatening me?' asked Steele.

'Yes,' said Steve. 'I am.'

Steele bit his teeth together, but he didn't say anything.

'So shall we play then?' Steve asked Steele.

'You don't think you've really got a chance, do you?' Steele smirked.

Steve winked at him. 'There's always a chance.'

Steele laughed. 'It's people like you who I blame for the problems with this world. With your namby-pamby "there's no losers" attitude. That's not real life. You're not preparing these kids for real life. You've even got a girl playing for you!'

Logan and his mates laughed.

Laura scowled at them.

'They want to play,' Steve said firmly. 'And you, nor anyone else, has the right to stop them.'

'So be it,' Steele sighed.

'Why don't we make it interesting?' asked Steve. 'If my lot win, you give them another shot at the school team.' Steve fixed his rival with a firm stare with his head tipped to the side, waiting for a response.

Steele looked around at the Freaks. He smirked. 'Right you are,' he said. 'But if my lot win, what do I get?'

'Five hundred quid,' Steve said.

'Dad,' whispered Seth. OK, they weren't poor, but his dad didn't have that kind of money to throw about.

Steele grinned. 'You're on.' He held out his hand.

Steve looked at it for a moment.

Seth thought his dad might spit on it.

Steve didn't spit on Steele's hand though. He shook it.

'Right,' said Steele. 'Let's get this started. Boys, this way.' Steele led his team away from the Freaks along the side of the pitch.

Logan winked at Seth as he went off.

Seth gave Logan a snarl.

Steve was shaking his head.

'Is there any need for those shorts?' he asked.

The Freaks laughed.

'Dad, you can't bet that much money,' Seth said.

'Yeah, Stevie, you can't,' Angelo added.

'It's just money,' Steve told them. 'I believe in you lot.'

'You sure?' Seth asked him. 'It's a lot of money.'

Steve nodded slowly.

'I'm sure. Right then, team. Are we ready?'

Seth nodded. Who knew what was going to happen to the Freaks after this? It could be the springboard for greatness or it could be the blow that destroyed them before they'd even really started. Seth did know that he was scared. The acid in his stomach was bubbling. His heart was pounding. He was so nervous, his sweat was sweating.

This was it.

'Go on then,' said Steve. 'Get in your positions. And remember. Play your stuff!'

The Freaks went onto the field.

Seth stood by the centre circle. He looked around at his team-mates. No one was smiling any more. Well, no one except Alan. Even Angelo's usual grin wasn't there. Seth was pretty sure his team were feeling the same nerves as he was.

'Have we really got a chance, Seth?' asked John.

'Yeah, course,' said Seth. 'You heard my dad. There's always a chance.'

Logan led his team onto the field and they took their positions. There were all smiling. They looked calm, relaxed and confident. They all had tans and nice haircuts. Except for Luke

Foreman. They looked like a boy band straight off *X Factor*. The Freaks looked more like one of the weirdo groups who got laughed at and kicked out in the early stages of the show. But Seth already knew that. It was the whole idea behind the team.

Steve joined the two captains in the centre circle. He pulled out a coin. 'Heads or tails?' he asked.

'He can choose,' said Logan.

'Heads,' Seth said.

Steve tossed the coin. He caught it and slapped it on the back of his hand. 'Heads.'

'We'll kick off,' Seth told them.

'Good luck,' said Logan, with a smirk.

John joined Seth at the centre spot.

Steve blew his whistle and the match kicked off.

Seth knocked it to John.

John knocked it back to Laura.

The school team were on her straight away, pressing hard.

'COME ON,' shouted Steele. 'GET THAT BALL! SHE'S A FLAMING GIRL!'

Laura snarled. She spun around with the ball, looking for space. There was nothing. She knocked it back to Angelo.

The ball was stolen away by Liam Boyle and

played through to Logan.

Logan cut in from the left, beating Ryo for pace. He went to the right and took the ball to the left, leaving Alex standing.

Beefy charged in.

Logan tried to dodge the challenge, but failed. Beefy left him in a heap in the box. Logan picked himself up quickly and threw his hands in the air.

Steve blew the whistle and pointed to the spot.

'THAT'S THE ONE!' shouted Steele. He clapped his hands.

Elle and the other girls from Seth's form cheered.

Seth groaned. 'Thanks, Dad!'

'Sorry, son,' said Steve. 'But I've gotta call it.'

Beefy picked himself up. He looked around at the other Freaks who'd gathered in a group on the edge of the box.

'Sorry.'

'At least you took him out!' said Angelo.

Logan put the ball down on the spot.

'Sam'll save it,' said Laura. 'COME ON, SAM!'

'You reckon?' Logan called over. He ran at the ball. Then he paused.

Sam dived to his right.

Logan dinked the ball over Sam as he

stretched for it in vain.

The ball bounced over the line and rolled across the grass behind.

One-nil to the school team.

Logan ran off with his finger over his mouth. The rest of his team ran after him.

Steele and the kids on the touchline cheered.

Seth turned away and trudged back to the centre circle.

Within minutes of the kick-off it was two. Mendes curled a peach from the edge of the area. Even Seth clapped. The Freaks weren't even getting a kick. Logan made it three with a header from a corner. Just before half time, Foreman added a fourth, after Logan had danced through the Freaks' defence and laid it off.

Steve blew the whistle for half-time.

The Freaks gathered in a group at the side of the pitch.

Steve joined them. 'What's the matter?' he asked.

'I don't know if you've noticed,' said Seth. 'But they're a little bit better than us.'

'So what if they are?' Steve replied. 'You're not playing your own game.'

'How can we play our game when we're losing four-nil?' asked Beefy.

'It's about you lot showing that lot that you ARE a team,' Steve told them. 'Use each other. Get stuck in. Don't be afraid to try things. Curtis, use your pace. Jordan, use that lovely right foot of yours. Seth, fight for the ball.'

'I'm trying!' Seth protested.

'Are you? Because it looks to me like you're scared. You're all scared. Don't be. It doesn't matter. There's nothing to lose here.'

'What about your money?'

'That's just some daft bet.' Steve shrugged. 'You don't need to worry about that. You don't need to worry about anything. Just play your game and enjoy it. Can you do that for me?'

Seth looked around at everyone. No one looked like they were enjoying themselves. In fact, each of them looked like they were in pain. This wasn't fun. He looked over at Logan's team.

Even though they were winning, Steele was shouting at them.

Logan blew Seth a kiss.

Seth was getting tired of Logan winking and blowing kisses at him. He wondered whether Logan fancied him a bit.

A GAME OF TWO HALVES

The teams took the field for the second half.

'COME ON!' shouted Laura.

'YEAH, COME ON!' Angelo bellowed. 'WE CAN DO THIS!'

Seth didn't know whether Angelo believed his own words, but he certainly didn't.

The school team kicked off. They started to knock the ball around at a leisurely pace. It was as if they thought they'd won already.

Seth felt a rising anger and it spurred him into action. He raced after the ball, but every time he got near one of their players, they just passed it around him. But he resolved to keep doing it. That's what his dad wanted. The Freaks had to at least work hard and hassle them. They weren't going to win the ball by standing and watching.

Seth was taking the lead and making himself a nuisance. He was quickly joined by Laura and

Angelo. Together, the three of them pressed the school team higher up the pitch.

Laura steamed in and stole the ball from Mendes before he could pass it. She knocked it out wide to Curtis.

He tore down the left, beating the right-back with a lucky flick. He played the ball into Seth.

Seth took the ball, spun around to goal. He looked up. Foreman was blocking his way, so he passed the ball to John.

John took a shot.

The ball sailed over the bar.

John burst out laughing. 'At least it was a shot!' he said.

They were all laughing.

Seth felt himself cheer up a bit. The tension and nerves had wound him up so tightly. The laughter did something to help him relax. It was just what they all needed, because from that point, the Freaks started to pass the ball better. They competed for the fifty-fifties. They even started having a few shots.

Then Jordan picked the ball up on the right. He beat the left back and cut in. He let fly with his right, striking the ball with the outside of his foot. The ball curled away from the keeper right into the top left of the goal. It was an absolute beauty.

Four-one.

The Freaks went wild.

Angelo went to give Jordan a hug, but Jordan just shook his head. Angelo hugged Alan instead.

With their mood lifted and a sudden injection of confidence, the Freaks *really* started playing. Their passes were coming off. Their tackling was tenacious. Their tricks were bamboozling the opposition.

Seth looked around at his team-mates. He wasn't sure how they'd managed it, but they all had a smile on their faces. They were enjoying it. They were playing their stuff. Just like his dad had said.

Angelo picked the ball up in midfield, just inside the school team's half. He looked up and hit a ball long. It sailed over Seth, heading for John.

John leapt into the air, towering way above the opposition's defence. He powered a header past the keeper.

Cracking goal.

Four-two.

Everyone chased after John.

Alan jumped up on his back and John gave him a piggy back down the length of the pitch! 'GIDDY UP, HORSIE!' shouted Alan.

Seth watched as Logan shouted at Boyle.

Boyle shouted back.

Steele shouted at all of them from the touchline. 'WHAT ARE YOU DOING?!'

On they went. After a shot from Hawksy, which Sam collected, Sam threw the ball out to Alan.

Alan knocked it inside to Beefy.

Beefy played it forward to Laura. She was immediately under pressure from Boyle. She knocked it back to Alex, who played it out to Ryo.

Ryo pushed forward with the ball. He dodged a challenge and played the ball inside to Angelo.

Angelo played a one-two with Laura, around Mendes and out to Jordan.

'GET THAT BLOODY BALL!' screamed Steele.

Jordan beat the full-back again. He whipped a wicked cross into the box.

John nodded it down to Seth.

Seth wanted to hit it first time, but he was confronted by Luke again. He looked around. Everyone was marked tight.

He played the ball out to Curtis.

Curtis raced at his man. He nutmegged the player, slipping the ball through to Alan who was running for the overlap.

Alan charged into the area. The ball wasn't

fully under his control. It wasn't even partly under his control. The ball bounced around in the area and somehow landed at Alan's feet. Five yards out. Not even Alan could miss from there.

'STOP HIM!' shouted Steele.

Alan swung at it.

Seth held his breath.

The ball flew between the posts.

Four-three.

'I SCORED!' shouted Alan. 'I SCORED!' He put his hands on his hips and kicked his feet out and started doing a little line dance.

It might not have been the best goal ever, but it was one of the best celebrations.

Every one of the Freaks copied Alan's dance. It was hilarious.

They all creased up.

Then John ran at Alan.

Alan raced away.

The whole team chased after Alan, but he dodged out of their way as they tried to grab him and pile on.

Eventually Alex managed to wrestle Alan to the floor and the whole team did pile on.

Alan screamed.

From the top of the pile, Seth looked around at the school team. He could see the fear in

Logan's eyes. He remembered that look. It was the way *his* team-mates had looked just before kick-off. And for once, he was looking over at Logan and his rival didn't have any smirks or smart comments to throw in his direction. That was a first.

Steele was jumping up and down, screaming his head off. He called Foreman 'Captain Caveman'. Mendes was 'frog eyes'. He even called Logan 'pretty boy sissy boy'. That was Seth's personal favourite.

We just might do this, thought Seth. At half-time, no one would've thought they could come back from four-nil down. But it was a real possibility now. And if they did, it would be legendary.

SETH'S BIG CHANCE

The third goal sparked them into life, because Logan's team started shouting at each other, trying to get themselves going, playing the way they'd played in the first half. They began to take control of the game again, putting passes together and dominating possession.

Mendes hit one from thirty yards out.

Sam just about tipped it over.

The corner came in.

Foreman powered a header at goal.

Sam pushed it wide.

'How long left?' Seth asked his dad.

Steve looked at his watch. 'Couple of minutes.'

Another corner came in.

Beefy headed it clear, but only as far as Logan.

He controlled the ball on his chest and unleashed a mean right foot volley.

The ball smacked against the bar.

Alex tried to get his head on it, but Boyle

shoulder-charged him.

Boyle laid the ball off to Mendes.

Mendes knocked it on to Logan.

Logan had another shot at goal. Just wide this time.

Time was running out. There wasn't long left to grab an equaliser, let alone a winner.

Sam blasted the ball up-field towards John.

John flicked it on, but the keeper came out and collected it.

In a flash, the ball was being blasted back up the other end.

Boyle won it in the air, knocking it down to Mendes.

Mendes shaped to shoot, but dummied it. He laid it off to Logan.

Logan beat a challenge from Angelo. He struck another shot at goal.

Sam dived low to his left. He stretched his arm and tipped it around the post.

The Freaks were coming under some real pressure now.

Corner to Logan's team.

'COME ON, YOU TOERAGS!' shouted Steele.

Seth might've laughed if he hadn't felt so anxious.

The school team all came up for it, leaving only their left-back back on the centre circle.

Seth stayed up too, figuring that if his team could clear the ball he might be one-on-one.

Mendes knocked the corner in.

Sam came off his line. He flapped at the ball, but somehow managed to gather it into his body. He hurled the ball up the field.

Seth controlled it on his chest in the centre circle. He brought it down, turned and went to the right, then cut back to the left, taking the ball past the left-back.

'TAKE HIM DOWN!' Steele screamed.

Seth knew the defender was chasing him. As he ran he remembered how Steele had said he was too slow.

There was no way he was going to let the defender catch him. Not this time. He raced with the ball, as fast as he could.

The defender was breathing down his neck and now the keeper was coming at him too.

This was it. The last kick. If he could score from here, he'd earn his team a draw. A draw no one would ever have thought was possible at half time.

The keeper charged towards Seth and slid in with a two-footed challenge.

Seth flicked the ball over him and jumped the tackle.

The keeper collided with the left-back, leaving

them both in a heap.

Seth had the goal at his mercy.

The ball bounced up.

This was it.

His Big Chance.

This was the moment he'd dreamed of. This was where he'd score the goal that mattered. This was where he would be declared the hero – King of the School.

He swung at it.

He hit the ball hard.

All around him, everything was in slow motion.

His head was filled with gurgled sounds of his team-mate's cheers.

The cries from Logan's teams.

The shouting and screaming from Steele and Elle and the other kids from school.

It had to be a goal.

Had to be.

There was no way he could miss.

No way.

The ball flew over the crossbar.

Worst.

Miss.

Ever.

Seth's dad blew the whistle for full time.

Seth collapsed in a heap on the ground. He

could hear the school team screaming and celebrating. He stared up into the blue sky above him, dizzy and dazed. His mind was a swirl of thoughts and feelings. They'd been so close to pulling off something really amazing and he'd let them down. He'd blown it so badly. He felt like he might cry. He was a full-blown ten on the suck-o-meter. His heart was in his bum like never before.

He lay on the ground, delaying the moment when he would have to see the looks on his team-mates' faces and know it was all his fault. The disappointment was so raw that it hurt, but despite that Seth realised he'd really enjoyed that second half. Jordan's goal was epic. He'd enjoyed John's towering header. He'd LOVED Alan's little line dance.

He burst out laughing.

A hand appeared in front of him.

Seth took it.

Jordan helped him to his feet.

Seth was still laughing.

Jordan patted him on the back. 'Unlucky, man.'

Seth shook his head 'That was terrible.'

'It was pretty bad,' said John.

'Not as bad as yours at the start of the half!' Curtis said.

The team gathered around. They were all laughing.

'And I didn't even strangle anyone!' said Angelo.

Steve joined them. 'Well played,' he said. 'Second half, you were brilliant.'

Seth looked around at his team-mates. They all still had big smiles on their faces. 'Yeah,' he said. 'We were, weren't we? And what about Alan's goal?'

Angelo grabbed Alan in a headlock and tousled his hair. 'What a goal, man! What a goal!'

'What about his dance!' Alex cried.

Alan put his hands on his hips and kicked his feet out. 'This one, you mean?'

Angelo copied him.

So did Beefy.

They all performed the line dance once again.

'How's it go?' asked Steve. He watched Alan for a moment, then joined in too.

They were all laughing and smiling.

'You did yourselves proud,' Steve told them, once they'd stopped dancing. 'You showed twice as much heart as that lot. That's what it's all about. Now, who are you?'

'FREAKS!' the whole team shouted together.

Steele came over to Seth and his team-mates. His face was still red from all the shouting and bawling he'd been doing. 'Ahh,' he said. 'Close, but not close enough.'

'We enjoyed that, didn't we, team?' said Steve.

The Freaks cheered again.

Steele sniffed and sucked his teeth.

'Don't worry, I'll get that money to you tomorrow,' Steve told him.

'About that,' Steele said. 'You know, if your boys still want to try out for the school again, I'd be happy to give them another shot.'

'You hear that?' asked Steve. 'He thinks you're good enough for the school team after all. What do you think?'

Seth looked around at his friends.

Angelo's face was screwed up.

Beefy shook his head.

'Na, we're good.'

Steele blinked. Then he turned and walked away, scratching the back of his neck as he went. He led the school team off the field. 'YOU CALL THAT DEFENDING?' he shouted as they made their way across the field.

Seth caught Logan's eye again. This time there was no mouthing of the word 'freaks', no winks or kisses. Instead, Logan gave a little nod.

Seth nodded back. The Freaks might have lost, but they did their best and they'd had fun. It felt like they'd won.

'Now,' said Steve. 'Who fancies some pizza and PlayStation?'

The Freaks cheered.

As they made their way across the field, Seth walked next to his dad. 'Sorry about missing,' he said.

'Are you crazy?' Steve replied. 'That was a great game. Best game I've seen all season.'

'Worth five hundred quid?' asked Seth.

'Worth every penny. You did me proud.' He tousled Seth's hair.

Seth smiled at him. He had the Best Dad in the world.

WHO WANTS TO BE A FREAK?

At school the next day, Seth and Freaks United were the talk of Year Seven. In fact, they were the talk of the whole school. As they walked to their form room, kids congratulated them, gave them pats on the back and high-fived them. Seth had always wondered what it would feel like to be popular in high school. Now he knew. It felt pretty cool.

They passed Jordan and Laura in the corridor.

'Training next week?' Laura asked.

'Damn straight,' said Angelo.

Jordan nodded. 'I haven't forgotten about that twenty quid,' he said.

Seth smiled and nodded.

Laura and Jordan carried on along the corridor.

'Do you reckon those two are going out now?' asked Beefy.

'Probably,' said Seth. He sighed.

Beefy and Angelo sighed too.

Alan didn't sigh. His eyes lit up. 'Does that mean Jordan will be my brother, after they get married? I've always wanted a brother!'

Elle and a group of girls walked past them. They giggled and whispered to one another. Elle smiled at Seth.

Seth frowned for a moment. Then smiled back.

'Were those girls checking us out?' asked Beefy, once he was sure they wouldn't hear him.

'Dunno,' said Seth.

'Definitely!' said Angelo.

'You reckon?' asked Seth.

'They totally were!' said Alan.

Seth laughed and slapped Alan on the back.

'Yo, Freaks!' shouted someone.

Seth turned around.

Logan, Mendes and Foreman were coming towards them.

'Looks like trouble, boys,' said Angelo. 'Don't worry, I'll count to ten.'

'Look,' Seth said to Logan. 'We don't want any trouble.'

'Neither do we,' said Logan.

Seth looked around at his mates with a frown. 'Well, what do you want then?'

'We were... we were wondering...' said Logan.

WHO WANTS TO BE A FREAK?

'If we could... you know... play for your team?'

Seth blinked, then scratched his head. He turned around to his mates.

They were all wide-eyed.

Beefy's mouth hung open.

Angelo and Alan were grinning.

'What do you think?' whispered Seth.

'Dunno,' said Beefy. 'They're not really... freaks... are they?'

Seth nodded. He turned back to Logan and his mates. 'You're not really what we're looking for,' he said. 'But we'll think about it.'

'OK, cool,' said Logan. 'Let us know, yeah?'

'Yeah, OK,' Seth told him.

Mendes and Foreman nodded and they all walked on.

'You know,' said Angelo. 'I might like high school after all!'

The four of them laughed.

Alan put his hand in. 'Come on,' he said. 'Can we do it right now?'

Seth cocked his eyebrow. He looked at Beefy, then Angelo. 'What you reckon? All in?'

Angelo grinned.

Beefy nodded.

Seth put his hand in. So did the others.

'On three,' said Alan. 'One. Two...'

The four of them shouted 'FREAKS!' together.

'We're never doing that again, by the way,' said Seth, once they were done.

'What? Never?' asked Alan.

'Never ever,' said Seth. He put his arm around Alan and smiled as the lads walked down the corridor.

A NOTE FROM JOHN

I really hope you enjoyed *Freaks United*. How about sharing it with your friends? If you're not already a member of a book club, why not join, or even start, one? Book clubs can be great fun, and they give you a chance to talk about all the things you did (or didn't!) like about a book.

Here are a few suggestions of what to think about to get you going. (Of course, you don't have to be in a book club – you can just do it for fun!)

The book's title…
- What did you think about this book when you first saw it?
- Did you realise it was about football? If you didn't, when you did realise, what did you think?
- Do you think 'Freaks United' was a good name for the team? Why/why not?
- If you were to start your own football team, what would it be called?

Seth and his mates were treated pretty badly by Mr. Steele.
- Do you think Mr Steele is unnecessarily cruel? Why?

- Does Mr Steele's behaviour sound familiar to you?
- If they hadn't been labelled 'freaks', do you think Seth and his friends would have gone on to form their own team?
- Do you think that Mr Steele's attitude was the main reason for Seth wanting to form their own team, or were there other reasons?

How would you react if you were told you weren't good enough to do something that you really wanted to do?
- Think about some of the things that Seth, Beefy and Angelo and Alan do to get the team together. Do you think that their plans were good? Or not?
- What would you do to get a team together?
- Do you think it's OK to have to do stuff for other people to get them to do something for you?

Seth comes up with the idea of starting the team, but others are also important in making it happen.
- Could Seth have done what he did without them?
- Would you like Seth as a friend?
- What did you think of the other characters – Beefy, Angelo, Alan, Laura and the others?

- Do you have a favourite? If so, why?
- Who are you most like? Would you have joined the Freaks?
- Did your view about any of the characters change by the end of the book?

Do you think it was right that things turned out the way they did?
- Did you feel sorry for the Freaks? Why/why not?
- What did you think would happen at the end of the story? Were you right?
- What was your favourite part of the book, and why?
- Was the book only about football, or were other things as, or more, important?
- What do you think Seth thought was the most important result of starting their own team?
- Do you have a dream? Have you thought about ways that you might achieve it?

Would you recommend *Freaks United*?
- Did you think *Freaks United* was funny?
- Which part made you laugh?